THE GIRLS OF CANBY HALL®

ONE BOY TOO MANY

EMILY CHASE

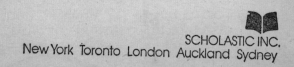

SCHOLASTIC INC.

New York Toronto London Auckland Sydney

ISBN 0-590-40343-5

12 11 10 9 8 7 6 5 4 3 2 1   11   6 7 8 9/8 0 1/9

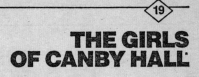

THE GIRLS
OF CANBY HALL

ONE BOY
TOO MANY

THE GIRLS OF CANBY HALL

CHAPTER ONE

Toby Houston sat on the edge of her bed in Room 407 and stared out the window as she pulled on her riding boots. Mostly she could only see the leaves of the giant trees in front of Baker House and a piece of the sidewalk that led on around the campus of Canby Hall School for Girls. She shook her head. You'd have to try hard to find any place more different from the Texas cattle ranch she had come from than this private boarding school in Massachusetts.

She jumped to her feet. She was homesick enough without letting herself think about it. With luck she could be dressed and gone before her two roommates, Andrea Cord and Jane Barrett, got back from their classes. Not that it was altogether luck that she had beaten them back to the room. She'd done it deliberately, afraid they'd keep her from getting out fast. She had cut across the big oval park that lay between the Main Building and the

1

dorms, running past the wishing pool without even fishing out a penny to throw in.

What would she wish for, anyway? The only thing she wanted was to get out of her school clothes, into jeans, and out into the warm October sun.

She had always loved that particular fall month. She had been named October. Nobody ever used her whole name, but she was named for the month she'd been born in and her birthday was only three weeks away. She couldn't even imagine that special day coming any place but at the ranch with her dad. He'd miss it, too, she knew he would. Since her mother had died, there had only been the two of them and they had become best friends.

Not that she had any other friends back home. When you live twenty miles out of Rio Verde, Texas, and ride a school bus back and forth every day, you couldn't make many friends if you wanted to!

Covering her tangle of red curls with the worn Stetson her dad had given her, she took the wide wooden stairs of Baker House two at a time. Three girls coming up the steps pulled back against the wall to let her clatter past.

"Howdy," one of them drawled in an exaggerated Texas accent. Toby felt her face redden. Okay, so she *was* a Texan and talked funny. Okay, so she *looked* ten miles tall in skinny-legged jeans and boots, especially with that cowboy hat perched on top of her head. She was about to snap back when she caught the girl's eye and realized the greeting had been friendly and just in fun.

"Howdy, yourself, you-all," she drawled, her green eyes dancing at how her dad would howl to hear her clowning like that. But there was a lot about Canby Hall that would surprise her dad.

Hadn't he asked for surprises by sending her away? The last thing she had wanted to do was leave him, her horse, her seven cats, and the endless starry skies above their ranch. In a way, she had felt betrayed by his decision. She had always figured they were a team. Does one member of a team send the other off somewhere she doesn't want to go? Not on your life.

Toby ran down the front steps and cut across the campus to get to the main road. She had tried to describe her roommates to her dad when she first came, but finally tore the letter up. At first it had been too awful to tell *anyone* about.

From the moment she got in late that first night, she had felt about as welcome as a snake in a picnic basket. That was all right. She didn't want to be there any more than her new roommates wanted her.

Jane Barrett was the worst. This was her second year at Canby Hall and she had asked for a single room because her first roommate, a girl named Gigi Norton, had made her life miserable. Jane was sure she had the room to herself until Toby and Andy were put in with her. The headmistress at Canby Hall, an elegant, cool woman named Patrice Allardyce, had said they had been matched by a computer. That was a laugh! They could have run a contest and not found three girls so completely different!

Jane was from Boston, a rich, cool girl with beautiful long blond hair. Andrea Cord was black and from Chicago. Andy was as neat as Jane was messy. Andy's clothes were as sharp and up-to-date as Jane's were preppie. Then there was Toby herself.

When Toby finally wrote her dad, she just told him their names and where they came from. She hadn't told him Andy was black. She had never really known a black girl before. There was something so special about this new experience that she didn't want to spoil it by putting it into the wrong words, even to her dad.

She would have made it back home to Texas by now, too, except for Andy and Jane. They had caught her just short of taking a bus back home. They had talked her into staying at Canby Hall and "learning to get on with humans," even if horses were better company than most of the people she'd met so far

Most people, but not all. Randy Crowell, for instance. Just thinking about Randy brought a strange little pain to her chest. He wasn't anything like the ranch boys she had ridden with on the bus back home. He wasn't like her dad or any of the hands who worked the ranch. And whatever was different about him made her think about him all the time.

Randy Crowell lived with his folks on their horse farm down the road from Canby Hall. Toby knew he was at least four years older than she was because he had dated Dana Morrison, whose sister Maggie was in 409 just next door. Dana had lived in 407 the year before, had graduated, and was now off in Hawaii with her father and stepmother. But Randy didn't act old, just great, and Toby found herself thinking about him an awful lot.

When Toby saw the roof of the Crowell barn in the distance, she cut across the fields to get there quicker. She stopped at the pasture where the horses usually grazed, and studied the empty field with a sinking heart. The horse she sometimes rode wasn't there, and neither was Randy Crowell. But at least there was open sky above the pasture. The sky in Texas was so big it tucked under the edges of the horizon. The campus of Canby Hall had big brick buildings and giant trees from the last century that cut off the view of the sky. You had to look straight up to see blue!

"I hate that place," she told herself. "I hate that place like thunder." She sighed. That wasn't true anymore, not since she and her roommates were becoming friends. What she hated was thinking about Randy and then not being able to see him.

* * *

Andrea Cord wasn't sorry to find the room empty. She had to memorize a poem for English and this gave her a head start.

Andy looked around the room and smiled. There was no doubt that three very different girls lived in this small space. The windows next to Jane's bed had pale ivory curtains and her bed was covered with an antique cross-stitched quilt. The blue and gray Persian rug on the floor next to her bed went perfectly with the Wedgwood blue walls of the room. Andy's bed was covered with a bedspread of a modern print of diagonal earth tone stripes, and there was a matching throw rug on the floor. And Toby's part of the room had a bed covered with a green army blanket, a Navaho rug on the floor and, over the bed was a teabag hanging from the ceiling. An object that Toby never explained to the girls. She had taken it down once, and then mysteriously had put it back, still not explaining what it meant.

After hanging up her school clothes, Andy put on hot pink leotards with bright warm-up socks. She propped her American lit book on a chair, and was whispering the lines out loud to herself and doing her stretch exercises when Jane Barrett came in. Andy grinned up at Jane and shoved back the pink headband holding her hair. She knew her cheeks gleamed with sweat from her exercise and she stifled a sigh. Jane, with her elegant face and long curly blond hair, always looked every inch the proper Bostonian lady that she was.

Even her clothes were restrained — a dove gray pleated skirt with a cashmere sweater and wool blazer.

In spite of her looks, Jane went through a room like a maintenance man spreading salt on an icy Chicago sidewalk. She dropped her jacket inside the door, dumped her books on Andy's desk, and had already thrown her scarf across the bed before Andy could say hi.

Jane smiled in that controlled way that looked snobbish if you didn't know her. "Toby around?" she asked.

"Come and gone," Andy told her, nodding toward the stack of books on Toby's desk. "My guess is that she's out looking for trouble."

At Jane's astonished glance, Andy shrugged. "Randy Crowell," she explained.

A little frown line appeared between Jane's eyebrows. "Randy seems nice enough."

"Plenty nice," Andy agreed. "But I think Toby has fallen for him. Notice how absent-minded she is? Dreamy, kind of."

Jane flushed. "There's nothing wrong with liking a nice guy."

"Not if he likes you back," Andy said. "But Randy treats Toby like my brother Charlie treats my baby sister Nancy. He does everything but pat Toby on her head."

"He *is* older," Jane agreed thoughtfully.

"He knows it, too," Andy said, leaning to catch her toes with one hand and then the other. "I'd just hate to see Toby hurt."

Jane plumped up a pillow and sat against it, shaking her head as she watched Andy stretch. "What energy," she sighed. "What in the world drives you to it?" As she spoke, she opened her notebook and took out her pen.

"Auditions," Andy gasped when she caught her breath. "Didn't you see the posters about the auditions for a holiday musical?"

Jane frowned. "I guess not." She closed the notebook over her finger. "Shelley Hyde, one of the girls who used to be in this room, was just fantastic in the play they put on last year. But everyone was really good. I wonder if the Oakley Prep guys will be in it again?"

Andy nodded. "So I hear."

Oakley Prep. Andy hadn't seen the nearby boys' private high school, but she'd heard about the mixers the two schools had on and off. Andy also kept hearing such great things about the boys from Oakley Prep that she couldn't help being curious.

That was something she'd have to check out for herself. Maybe she would get to the Harvest Moon dance coming up at Oakley Prep at the end of the month. And maybe not. The only Oakley Prep boy she knew was Jane's friend, Cary Slade, who was lead guitarist in the Oakley Prep rock group, Ambulance.

Jane was still watching her. "I sure hope you get a part, Andy. Toby and I will be your cheering section."

Andy crossed her ankles and looped her arms around them. Cheering section. Boy, did that make her think of Chicago! She could still see the theater lights dimming as she came on stage for her first solo dance recital back home. Her family had filled an entire row. Her dad had even left his restaurant in charge of a friend to come with her mom and brothers and baby sister, Nancy, to see her dance. She grinned, remembering her younger brother Ted's excited voice when the final dance was over. "That's my sister," he had cried over the rising applause of the audience.

Jane was frowning and writing in her notebook when Andy finished exercising. It impressed Andy that Jane worked as hard at her creative writing class as Andy did at her dancing. It couldn't be as exciting! She hadn't been able to think about anything else since she saw the announcement about the musical. She would get a part; she had to. Some day she was going to be a prima ballerina. She could even see the headline in *The Chicago Tribune:* Chicago-born Andrea Cord Dazzles Them in *Swan Lake*.

The rap at the door startled Andy back to reality and brought Jane's head up out of her notebook.

"Your phone is out of order. There's a call for Barrett downstairs," someone called in. Andy watched Jane's face bloom with delight as she tumbled off the bed. When the girl at the door added, "Long distance," Jane's face fell.

Andy watched Jane sigh as she put her

notebook down. Although Canby Hall was totally different from Chicago, the boy-girl problems were just the same. Boyfriends only came two ways . . . feast or famine. While Toby Houston couldn't get Randy Crowell's attention, Jane not only had Cary Slade on her mind but still had a boyfriend back in Boston who kept calling her as if he owned the phone company.

Andy had really done a double take when she first saw Cary Slade. He was such a typical rock-and-roller — long brown hair, a single earring, and a tight wiry build. Even his clothes would have fit in with Chicago groups — grungy jeans, leather jacket, and boots. But he wasn't as typical as he looked. According to Dee Adams, next door, he was from a famous old family and was rebelling with his music. But wherever he came from, he was an unlikely guy for Jane!

Andy watched Jane go out the door looking like a condemned woman walking her last mile. In spite of his name, this guy in Boston, Cornelius Worthington III, *couldn't* be as stuffy as Jane made him sound. Andy caught Jane's eye and grinned encouragement.

"If that long distance call it from Baryshnikov, it's for me," she kidded Jane.

Jane's smile was a little strained, but it *was* a smile.

CHAPTER TWO

Toby Houston leaned against the fence that enclosed Randy Crowell's horse pasture. The green was fading from the grass, glinting it with gold. October. Even if it weren't her very own month, she was sure she would have loved it best. The sky was an intense blue above the empty fields. Along with the bird songs from the nearby woods she heard the hammering of the workers who were putting up new stables beside the Crowell barn.

Leaning her weight on one hand, she vaulted the fence and ran toward the sound. The knee-high grass whispered against the leather of her boots. Even if she didn't see Randy, it would be more fun to see how the work was progressing on the stables than to go back to the dorm and be trapped inside a room again.

The building was already framed in, with hollow rectangles where the windows and doors would go. Inside, workers were building horse stalls with pale, sweet-smelling lumber. When Toby stepped through the open doorway, two men looked up. One was a stranger to her, but Randy had introduced her to the older man, Bert, who worked on the ranch.

"Hi there, Texas," Bert said, grinning up at her. "You just missed Randy. He went off to play tennis with a buddy."

"Tennis!" she said in amazement. "Why would he want to chase a ball around on a day like this, when he could ride horseback?"

Bert laughed. "He probably has to flip a coin every time he gets a free hour this time of year. But there are good riding days all winter. There aren't that many days left for him to play tennis outdoors."

Toby sat on her heels in the doorway. Back home in Texas, they called that "hunkering." It felt like home to linger there in the door of the stable and watch Bert and his companion fit the boards in place and then nail them down with rhythmic hammer strokes.

When the joint was finished, Bert got up and stretched, arching his back. "If Randy gets back early enough for a ride, I'll tell him you stopped by."

Toby got up, too, suddenly feeling shy. "I'd appreciate that. Tennis! It really surprises me that Randy's so crazy about that game."

"Folks tend to like doing things they do well," Bert said, nodding. "Randy does two things better than almost anyone else. Ride horses and play tennis."

"I wouldn't argue with you about the horses," she admitted. "But *tennis!*"

Toby walked back to Canby Hall slowly. There had to be more to the game of tennis than she had ever seen. She couldn't imagine Randy being caught up with something as silly as tennis *looked* to her. She had never even picked up a tennis racket that she could remember. You don't see many tennis courts on cattle ranches. She plucked a dry straw of pasture grass and chewed it thoughtfully. Maybe she should give the game a try. If she did happen to like it, she would have one more thing in common with Randy.

After Jane Barrett replaced the hall phone, she stood a long time with Neal's voice echoing in her head. He had been cheerful enough when the conversation began, but the way he had said good-bye could only be called sullen.

Dee Adams' voice broke into her thoughts. Jane turned to see Maggie Morrison's roommate studying her with a concerned expression. "Nothing wrong, I hope," Dee said.

Jane shrugged and managed a weak smile. "Not really. I just don't want to go to Boston this weekend."

Dee raised her shoulders in an exaggerated gesture that made her long blond hair tumble over them. Jane had always heard about "California girls" but had never known one

until she met Dee Adams. She had been prepared for Dee's golden tan, the sun glints in
her hair, and the casually outrageous way she
dressed. But she hadn't expected Dee to be as
outspoken as she was, as open about her
opinions, whether you asked her or not. More
than once Dee had come out with things that
made Jane gasp.

"Boston," Dee repeated. "That sounds like
heaven to me. It's a good thing I didn't get
that call. I'd be gone, out the door, packed
away by sundown. Boston has to beat this
Nowhere City for excitement. Lights. I bet
they have bright lights at night, and I *know*
it's on the ocean. How could you possibly
turn down a chance to escape?"

Jane smiled to herself. Dee made everything sound as exciting and colorful as she
was. The immense shirt Dee had belted
around her slender waist was the same strong
bright blue as her eyes and her hair shone
mixed gold in the light.

"Let's just say I don't want to go," Jane
said.

Dee fell into step with Jane as she walked
toward Room 407. "Well, if there isn't anything worth going for, that's a little different."

"That isn't exactly it," Jane admitted. "My
friend has bought tickets to a rock concert
and wants me to come down for it."

Dee whistled softly and looked at Jane's
face. "Hey!" she said. "Didn't your mother
teach you to take the cookies when they were

being passed? I would have gone in a minute."
She hesitated. "Unless I was hung up over
another guy." Then she nodded. "Of course,
that's it. That's a decent reason. It would be
pretty crummy to let him treat you to a concert while you're dating Cary Slade. I hope
he didn't take it too hard that you have a
new boyfriend."

As they reached the door of 407, Jane
turned to stare at Dee in astonishment. "I
didn't tell him."

Dee stared at her. "You just gave him some
made-up excuse instead of the truth?"

Jane shook her head, feeling a rush of color
come to her cheeks. "I couldn't possibly tell
Neal about Cary. He'd never understand."

Andy, locked in a stretch position on the
floor, got into the conversation. "I thought
all boyfriends were born knowing they could
be replaced. This Neal of yours has to be
the original Boy-in-the-woods."

Jane wished she had never told Dee about
the call. "I don't want to talk about it," she
said firmly. "I just don't want to go to Boston
for a concert this weekend, and that's that."

"No mystery there," Dee said sarcastically.
"If I was lying to some nice boy, I wouldn't
want to talk about it, either."

"You don't know what you're saying," Jane
said, raising her voice without meaning to.
Dee could carry bluntness too far.

"I know what a lie is," Dee said. She turned
away with a disgusted look. "Andy," she said.

"Can I borrow your dictionary? Mine refuses to spell things the way I have them written."

Andy nodded and wagged her head toward the desk, where the dictionary stood neatly between her thesaurus and a history book. As Dee left she looked back at Jane, who was staring at her in disbelief. "Maybe you've got what it takes to write fiction. Good luck with your little plot."

In the shocked silence that fell after Dee was gone, Andy groaned. "That's all we need, another feud around here. I'm sorry I butted into your conversation, Jane. And I'm sorry I made that crack about guys. How you deal with Neal and Cary is your own business. But it doesn't seem like you."

"How isn't it like me?" Jane challenged her.

Andrea shrugged and pulled off her headband. "I don't know. I guess I think of you as being straight, really honest and fair."

"So now I'm not honest," Jane said, not even fighting her rising anger. "I can't win with you two."

"All I know is that you and Cary Slade like each other and you haven't told the boy back home about him," Andy said quietly. "That much I know isn't fair. Come on, Jane. I don't want to fight about it. It's your business."

"It *is* my business," Jane said. "But it would be nice if my friends tried to understand."

Andy looped her arms around her legs and

sighed. "Okay. I'll give it a real try." She looked up at Jane expectantly.

Jane hesitated. "It's different in Boston. People aren't as relaxed as you and Dee are. There's a right way and a wrong way to do everything."

"And not being honest is the right way?" Andy asked.

"You are *not* trying," Jane said. "Neal has been more than a boyfriend all these years. We grew up together. Our folks really expect us to be married some day. They don't say it like that, but Neal and I both know it."

"That kind of thing is ancient history," Andy said. "People don't do that anymore."

"Maybe it's ancient history to you," Jane said. "But Neal and I really get along. Sure he's stuffy but he was raised that way, just like I was. If I told Neal about Cary Slade, he would probably sulk all week and complain to everyone in sight."

"I don't know how you can care about a guy who would act like that. Or did you give him some real good reason to think you *were* his girlfriend? I mean that you wouldn't go out with anyone else."

"Not really," Jane said, hesitating a little. "Well, maybe. I did tell him I was crazy about that concert group, and I did promise I would come home for special things."

"Has he already bought the tickets? Those things cost a lot."

"He does have the tickets," Jane admitted. "But that's no problem for Neal, his parents paid for them."

Andy leaned to touch the toes of her left foot. "Then let his parents go to the concert with him."

Jane's angry look softened into a grin. "Now there's a picture! It's a *rock* concert, Andrea!"

"So?"

"So Neal's folks are as bad as mine, Andy. The last rock they were interested in was the one the pilgrims landed on at Plymouth."

Andy grinned. "Not bad, Jane, not bad."

Jane stared absently at the door. "I don't want to fight with Dee, but I get really mad when she's so rude and outspoken about someone else's business."

Andy didn't reply. Jane *was* being two-faced. That could hurt everybody in the end. Jane couldn't really expect anyone to approve of a girl who didn't have guts enough to be honest.

Andy felt a surge of relief to see Maggie Morrison's impish face peer in at the door. Maggie was more into teasing and fun than heavy scenes. Just seeing her eyes sparkling behind her little owl glasses cleared the air. Maggie was still wearing her crazy jeans jacket with slogans down the sleeves and a giant muffler that hung almost to her knees. Sometimes Andy wished she had known the "old girls" in 407 like Maggie did. From

things that Maggie had said, she knew she
would like them all — Dana, Maggie's sister,
Faith Thompson whose wonderful photographs Andy had seen, and Shelley Hyde who
sounded like a lot of fun.

Maggie staggered in, holding a cardboard
box with both arms. "Package of bricks for
Miss Andrea Cord," she announced, groaning
at the end.

"Bricks?" Andy asked, springing to her feet.

"That's what it feels like," Maggie said.
Try it!"

Andy whistled at the weight of the box,
then broke into a grin. "Oh, Mom couldn't
have! It can't be what I think!"

Jane slid over to watch Andy cut off the
sealing tape. "She did! It is!" Andy squealed
as a card fell out inscribed, "Happy October!"

"Did what? Is what?" Maggie asked.

"Just look," Andy said, carefully pulling
back the wrapping.

A stunned silence filled the room. "Those
are the largest, most incredible candy apples
I have ever seen in my life!" Maggie
breathed.

"Chicago style," Andy crowed. "Just like
Marshall Fields makes them."

"But they're immense!" Jane protested.
"Who could ever take a bite out of something
like that?"

Andy pulled her letter opener from her
desk drawer. She sliced one of the apples into

wedges, then handed the pieces around. With a look of pure ecstasy, she bit into her own piece of crisp, candy-coated apple.

Maggie did the same only to find herself unable to speak with her mouth filled with firm caramel.

"We think big in Chicago." Andy grinned at her. "But we do try not to bite off more than we can chew!"

Jane looked at her with swift suspicion. Was she talking about the apple or Jane's boyfriend problem? Andy's face was the picture of innocence, so Jane couldn't tell.

Dusk was settling in by the time Toby reached the campus of Canby Hall. Twilight came early under Canby Hall's great trees, which had been growing there since the school was founded in 1897. A flock of migrating geese honked and splashed on the pond that little Julia Canby had skated on as a child. Lights shone through the trees from the huge house where the headmistress, Patrice Allardyce, lived.

Toby had heard kids scoff about what a big fuss Ms. Allardyce and the staff made about the history of the school. Toby wasn't about to scoff. Though she'd never admit it, she never tired of looking up at the portrait of Julia Canby that hung on the wall of the Main Building.

History was important. Toby knew how proud she was that her very own ancestor,

Sam Houston, had been a part of the making of Texas. And the story of how old Horace Canby established the school in the memory of his little dead daughter, Julia, almost brought tears to her eyes. She could imagine her dad, if he was that rich, and if something happened to her, wanting to make her name live on the way Julia's did.

Toby took the path behind the library. Instead of going straight home to Baker House, she walked past Addison House to the tennis courts. She wove her fingers into the mesh of the wire fence, staring at the empty courts.

So you hit a ball across that net at the other player and he hit it back at you. She would get out there first thing in the morning and talk to the coach. If Randy cared enough to play tennis, well, there had to be *something* about the game that was worth her time, too.

Even if it was only that someday maybe she and Randy could play it together.

Jane and Andy were both piled on their beds looking miserable when Toby got in. They both shook their heads when Toby asked if they were ready to go down to dinner. "You must know what they're having," she accused them with quick suspicion. "Not that gray muck that slithers?"

Andy and Jane shook their heads as one. Then Andy pointed to the box on her desk. "Food from home," she said.

"Again?" Toby asked. She was continually

astonished at the stream of packages of food Andy's parents sent her. She would be lucky to get a box of candy in her birthday box. Her dad's idea of a present was a new saddle or a leather jacket. She looked at the single giant caramel apple left and whistled. "Don't tell me there were three of those monsters!"

Jane nodded and groaned. "Eat at your own risk!"

Toby looked over at Andy who was lying flat with both hands on her stomach. "Aren't you having auditions for the musical tonight?"

"Tomorrow," Andy said. "And is that a good thing! They didn't give the name of the production, but I doubt if it features the dance of a Caramel Apple Monster."

Toby peered at the apple again and shook her head. "There's no way I can face *that* on an empty stomach. I'll just go down and check out dinner."

Besides, she thought as she ran down the stairs two at a time, if she was going to become a tennis whiz, it was never too soon to start watching her weight.

CHAPTER THREE

After dinner Toby hadn't really been able to concentrate on her home work, thinking about Randy. The next day, for the first time since coming to Canby Hall, she was stumped by a pop test. She knew that Mrs. Offutt was going to put more red checks on that geometry paper than she'd ever seen before. But that was okay. Once she got the tennis business set up, she would put herself back on her normal study schedule.

She managed to concentrate during biology but when study hall time came, she lost her patience. The morning was half gone. She wasn't going to get a chance to talk to the coach unless she made one. She spread out her notebooks and started reading her American history assignment.

It was no good. Her restlessness grew as the study hall period dragged on. She watched one of the other students go up and start talking to the monitor. When they walked together to a reference shelf, Toby got up and slipped out the door at the rear of the room.

The minute she was outside, she was terrified. She walked around the park past Addison House, trying to look as official as possible in case she ran into anyone who knew her.

Girls in blue and gold Canby Hall sweat suits were playing on all eight tennis courts. The coach, with a whistle dangling from around her neck, stood outside the fence talking to a woman whose back was to Toby.

Toby watched the play with narrowed eyes. Dee Adams was playing on the third court against a tall brunette girl Toby didn't know. Dee served powerfully and made the game look easy enough. If Dee liked the game, that was another point in its favor. Dee was level and honest, for all that she sometimes came off a little bigger than life.

Toby knew so few girls by name that she was startled to see one she recognized. The girl walking back on the end court to retrieve a ball was Gigi Norton.

Gigi was different-looking enough to remember. Her build was athletic, short, and a little stocky with well-developed legs and wide hips. She had shiny black hair in a crisp stylish cut and might have been pretty if she hadn't worn so much makeup. Personally Toby, who had owned one lipstick in her whole life, hated that made-up look, with penciled brows and all that black lining around the eyes.

So far Toby knew more *about* Gigi Norton than she really knew *her*. Maggie had said right out that Gigi was the "most thoroughly rotten girl in Canby Hall." Jane, who would know Gigi the best, because she had roomed with her the year before, never said anything. But her lips tightened and she looked away when Gigi's name was mentioned.

When Gigi reached the fence she looked at Toby. Toby returned her gaze steadily, but felt uncomfortable under that measuring stare. Then Gigi, after shrugging, turned away with an insolent smile. Tennis had won a point with Dee, and lost one with Gigi in the same two minutes.

Toby had been too busy reacting to Gigi to see that the woman who had been talking with the coach was Patrice Allardyce. Neither had she seen her leave the coach and walk toward where Toby was standing. Toby's heart went right to her boots. Like every new girl at Canby Hall, Toby had met the headmistress right away. This beautiful, handsomely dressed, unsmiling woman had terrified her that first day. Maggie had later told her that Miss Allardyce had suffered some great tragedy years before and had never laughed since. Everyone had told her that the headmistress considered breaking a Canby Hall rule in the same class with high treason.

Patrice Allardyce, in a soft tweed suit in mingled shades of lavender with a silk blouse, made Toby feel like an absolute slob in her denim skirt and jacket. As Toby caught her breath, the headmistress spoke in a cool voice.

"Good morning, October. I didn't realize you were in this class."

"I'm not," Toby said hastily. "Or rather I want to be, but. . . ."

Miss Allardyce's clear eyes were icy on Toby's face. "Then if you are not in this class, you are presumably supposed to be somewhere else."

"I only came to speak to the coach," Toby stammered, feeling her face redden under the woman's level glance.

Miss Allardyce's perfectly groomed eyebrows rose and fell slowly like a barometer of her thoughts. "No Canby Hall girl would interrupt an instructor during her class period, would she, October?"

"No, ma'am," Toby said. "I guess not."

"Then I suggest you go to where you are *supposed* to be at this hour and make an appointment with the tennis coach at *her* convenience."

Toby nodded and walked away, feeling as awkward as a new colt with Patrice Allardyce's eyes following her. It's not as if I had cut a real class, Toby fumed inwardly. And with any luck at all, she could get back into study hall without having been missed.

She didn't have any luck at all.

The study hall monitor looked up as Toby slipped in through the back door. She looked at the sheet on her desk and made a notation on it. Toby knew she had written something beside her name. She wriggled in her seat for a long resentful moment before going up to the desk.

"Excuse me," she said. "I tried to get a chance to talk to the tennis coach. Miss Allardyce told me I should make an appointment." At the mention of the headmistress's name, the scowl on the monitor's face disappeared, as if it were chalk being rubbed from a blackboard.

"Did you get your appointment?" the monitor asked, suddenly almost cordial.

Toby shook her head. "I was due here so I thought I should come back."

The monitor nodded and looked at the clock. "If you hurry, you should be able to get over to the sports complex before your next class."

"Thank you," Toby told her, unable to meet the girl's eyes.

Andy could never remember a longer day in her entire life. The minutes dragged, refusing to add up to the hours that would bring the day to a close. By noon time her stomach was in such an upheaval that she was afraid to put more than a diet cola in it. She kept thinkingly longingly of her family and being annoyed with herself for doing it. She wasn't like Toby Houston, who would give anything to go back where she came from, or even like

Dee Adams, who considered Canby Hall "Dullsville" and missed the fun of her home in Laguna Beach. Andy had felt smothered at home and *wanted* to be off on her own. But now, with the auditions coming up, she could do with a little loving support. But it was silly to call all the way to Chicago long distance just because her knees felt wobbly.

She walked past the public phone booth three times before breaking down and placing the long distance collect call.

The operator rang the number at the Cord home nine times before Andy would let her give up. Then she called her father's restaurant. The minute she heard the background noise behind his voice, her heart fell. She hadn't even thought about what time it was. She heard peoples' voices, the clatter of dishes, laughter. It was twelve-thirty at Canby Hall. That made it eleven-thirty in Chicago, with the early lunch rush in full swing in her dad's restaurant.

Of course her father accepted the charges. "Andy, honey, are you all right?" he asked, before she could even say hello.

"I'm fine," she told him. "Where's Mom?"

"In the kitchen supervising. Now come on, baby, what's the matter? I know my girl wouldn't call unless she had a good reason. You feeling all right? Not sick or anything?"

"Not really," Andy hesitated. "I don't feel the best, but maybe I'm just scared to death."

His words came swift and concerned. "Scared of what, Andrea? What danger are you in?"

"Not danger," she told him. "It's just that . . . well I'm scared. I guess I could use a hug before I audition for this play this afternoon. Oh, Dad, what if I don't make it? What if I get up there and can't even dance?"

His laughter rang in her ears only a moment. "*You* not be able to dance? Why, Andrea Cord, I'm ashamed of you. All those butterflies you had in your stomach when you were five should have flown away by now. You're the best, girl, the living best. What kind of a thing is this again?"

"Audition," she mumbled, suddenly fighting tears at the love in his voice.

"Audition!" He said it in a way that made it sound as if she had the star role nailed down already.

The confidence in his voice made the things she wanted to say sound whimpery and baby-ish. "I don't have a chance to get the lead role because I'll be the only black face in the whole place," she said quickly. "If I don't get to dance in this musical, my heart will just break. I know it. Dad," she went on swiftly, "Dad, I'm scared! I'm really scared."

"My Andrea scared?" His tone turned to something like a pep talk. "This isn't like my Andrea. I must be talking to the wrong girl. My Andrea would never call up here with tears in her voice about dancing. My girl was born with wings on her feet. Wings . . . remember?"

She had to swallow to keep tears out of her voice. "I remember, Dad. But you cross your fingers, hear? And, oh, Daddy, I love you all so much."

She spent a long time in the wash room, rinsing her face with cold water to fade the red from her eyes. What a baby she had been to call and dump on her father like that. She could just hear him worrying about it to her mom back in the kitchen. She'd just have to remember his words to keep her going. As she splashed her face, she whispered, "Wings on my feet, wings on my feet."

By the time her English class was finished, she could hardly drag herself back to Baker House. After going up the stairs and into 407, she didn't even look around before setting her books on the desk. Only when she turned to lie down on her colorful bedspread did she see Toby flat on her back on her own bed, staring at the ceiling.

"Hey," Andy asked her. "What's up with you?"

"Nothing," Toby said sullenly. "Absolutely nothing. Everything's down."

"Including me," Andy said, stretching out on her own bed and closing her eyes.

"Maybe it's the weather," Toby suggested, peering over at her.

Andy shook her head. "It's me."

"Me, too," Toby agreed, rolling back to stare upward again at the tea bag hanging from the ceiling. Twilight settled into the room but neither of them got up to turn on a lamp.

Then Jane whirled in, her cheeks pink from the outside chill and her eyes glistening. She flipped on the light and stood staring at them. "Good grief!" she cried. "All you two need is a lily on your chests to make this place into a mortuary."

"Very funny," Toby said, shutting her eyes tightly against the sudden glare of light.

"Absolutely hilarious," Andy agreed, doing the same.

"Hey, guys," Jane coaxed. "Nothing can be that bad."

"Want to bet?" Toby asked. "I cut out of a study period, halfway lied to keep out of trouble, and then couldn't talk that stubborn coach into working with me."

Jane looked at her a moment and then turned to Andy. "And you?"

"I blew every class all day, and then called my dad collect at prime time rates when he was at his busiest. . . just because I needed someone to tell me how great I am."

Jane sat on the edge of her bed. "Let's look at this in a less emotional way. Why won't the coach work with you, Toby?"

Toby flopped over angrily. "She says she needs every minute to get her team ready for fall competition."

"They teach tennis at the recreation department down in Greenleaf. The coach there is supposed to be really good. You might try that," Jane suggested.

Toby rose on her elbows to stare at Jane. "The recreation department? But do they have indoor courts?"

"I would guess they do," Jane said. "They were advertising winter tennis lessons in the town hall."

Toby grinned. "Jane, you're fabulous!" She swung her feet onto the floor. "I'll get right on it."

"Any magic words for me?" Andy asked without opening her eyes. "Do they have a sign posted in the town hall that all crybaby collect calls from Canby Hall are free in the month of October?"

Jane laughed softly. "You probably didn't even talk for three minutes. Anyway, your call probably made your Dad's day. Don't forget, I've met your dad and know how proud he is of you. All day long he's probably been telling people his Andrea is auditioning tonight."

Andy stared at her. "Barrett, you astonish me. There's really a brain under that mop of washed-out hair."

Jane laughed again and rose, just as Maggie rapped at the door and stuck her head in. "Want to walk over with me to the auditions, Andy?"

Andy stared at her. "Are you trying out, too? I didn't know you danced."

Maggie grinned in that impish way. "We can't all be stars! I love working backstage, painting scenery and prompting, whatever they'll let me do."

The auditorium looked different set up for the auditions. The room was half filled with both Canby Hall girls and boys from Oakley Prep who had come to try out. For the first ten minutes the uproar was terrible. "This place is as loud as the Loop when an el train is going over," Andy complained to Maggie.

When the director finally rapped for order, Andy's stomach gave one of those giant sickening thumps. She was absolutely certain it had landed upside down. She put her hand over her black leotards, trying to quiet the strange, churning feelings.

"We can't expect to finish casting in one night," the director shouted, "but let's get started."

During the tryouts, the room was plunged into darkness except for the brilliantly lit stage. There was something spooky about moving in that wavering line of girls and knowing you were being judged by someone sitting in the darkness beyond the footlights. Andy went through every dance step she had ever learned in that next two hours. The ballet steps were the hardest to execute on the crowded stage. But when she spun out alone, followed by a single radiant spotlight, she felt herself again . . . Andrea, with wings on her feet.

When it was over and she was mopping herself dry to start back home, she sought Maggie's eyes. "Did I do all right?"

"You were fabulous!" Maggie said.

"You wouldn't kid me?" Andy insisted.

Maggie shook her head. "You were one of the very best."

One of the very best. That wasn't good enough. She had to be the *absolute* best to get the leading role. She looked at Maggie but didn't dare ask.

"If you find your name posted on the board outside, you are to return for the second audition tomorrow night," the director said. "To the rest of you, thanks and better luck next time."

Andy dreaded going to the board as much as she ached to see the list. She waited until the crowd thinned out to go stare up at the handwritten names. Since they weren't in alphabetical order, she didn't see her own for a moment. Then it was there. Andrea Cord. As plain as day.

She had made it. She was halfway home.

Jane looked up from her books as Andy and Maggie walked in. "How did it go?" she asked.

"I survived the first audition," Andy told

her. "I might make it, Jane. I just might."

"Congratulations! If you survived the first audition you will at least get to dance in the chorus," Jane said.

Andy rebelled inwardly at her words. Just being in the chorus wasn't enough; she wanted the lead role. It didn't help that her own friends were saying things like "one of the best," and "dance in the chorus." Without changing into regular clothes, she picked her books up again.

"If anybody wants me, I'm in the library making up for a lost day," she said over her shoulder.

Maggie watched Andy leave without smiling.

"How was she?" Jane asked.

Maggie shook her head. "She really *was* one of the best," Maggie said.

"But not *the best*?" Jane asked.

"I won't be the one to pick the lead," Maggie said. "I just hate to see her have too high hopes."

"Well, anyway, Toby has solved *her* problem," Jane said. "She called from the rec department. She's getting her first tennis lesson tonight." She grinned. "My other news might not be important to anyone but me."

"That makes it important to me, too," Maggie said with a smile.

Jane tried to smile with pleasure, but she wasn't *really* smiling. "Cary asked me to be his date for the Harvest Moon Dance coming up at Oakley Prep."

"You don't look as happy as I thought you would," Maggie said.

Jane shook her head, pushing her long blond hair back. "Problems, always problems. Neal called again tonight. His prep school has scheduled their fall dance that same Saturday. He wasn't the world's best sport when I told him I couldn't go with him."

When Maggie said nothing, Jane looked up at her. "You are looking at me like Dee does."

Maggie shrugged, but before she could say anything, Jane was glaring at her. "Nobody around here is even trying to see my side of this. You all act as if I was some kind of monster. I just *can't* break off with Neal. We've been a duo since we were kids. Our parents. . . ."

"Let your parents go out together," Maggie said.

"You not only *act* like Dee, you *talk* like her, too. And Andy's just as bad!" Jane, her cheeks scarlet, turned toward the wall.

Maggie left silently, pulling the door shut behind herself. As she walked to her own room next door, she shook her head. She had often wondered if anything in the world would make Jane Barrett lose her cool. Maybe the answer was something as simple as a guilty conscience.

CHAPTER FOUR

On the second day of auditioning, Toby was up and out before Jane's alarm even went off. When Jane had showered and returned to the room, Andy still lay silent under her covers.

"It's almost eight," Jane told her.

"I can't stand another day like yesterday." Andy's voice came muffled through the sheet she had pulled over her face.

"Where do you suppose Toby is off to?" Jane mused, fishing her boots out of the closet.

"I wonder if professional dancers wake up with stomach aches every morning. I feel awful," Andy said.

"It feels colder this morning. What should I wear?" Jane asked.

"I don't think I'm going to make it until tonight," Andy said.

"Do you want me to set the alarm again before I go off to breakfast?" Jane asked.

Andy pulled the sheet down and sat straight up. "You don't even care how miserable I am," she said quietly. "You just go about your business, talking about the weather and alarms and not paying any attention to anybody but yourself. *Other* people have problems. But you don't care."

Jane stared at her a moment, her back stiffening. "I care as much about your problems as you do about mine," she said hotly. Then, without another word, she turned and left without resetting the alarm.

The minute Jane was gone, Andy leaped out of bed, sorry she'd been short with Jane. But Jane could be so . . . Jane. So aloof. She went into the bathroom down the hall and stood under the hot water a long time, trying to make the coldness in her bones go away. Just as she finally stepped out, she heard the shower next to hers turned on. From the jeans and flannel shirt wadded up on the floor Andy guessed the other girl was Toby, back from wherever she had disappeared to before either she or Jane wakened.

Andy stood a long time staring into her own closet and opening and shutting doors. Even the bright, warm colors she usually loved looked dull and lifeless to her. She needed something to cheer her up. She couldn't even borrow anything that was right. Jane's clothes were too drab and everything Toby owned looked Western. She gave up and was pulling on her pink lambswool sweater when Toby came into the room with her mop of red hair still dripping.

"Jane wondered where you had gone," Andy told her.

"I was working out on the backboard with my tennis racket," Toby explained.

"At dawn? Without any breakfast?" Andy asked.

Toby grinned at her. "You'd understand if you'd seen how badly I did at my lesson. Talk about not being able to hit the side of a barn. I couldn't have hit the Houston Astrodome with that silly little green ball. Something was wrong with either me or the racket. Even when I did connect with a ball, it never went where I wanted it to. Did Jane go down to breakfast?"

Andy nodded. "I guess so. She was really cool this morning."

Toby looked surprised. "How come?"

Andy grunted and pulled out her coat. "She doesn't have time for anybody but herself."

Toby stared at her. "How can you say that? Just last night she sat here and listened to both of us wail about our problems. She helped me and then tried to help you look at what had happened another way. If anybody ever lived up to 'A friend in need is a friend indeed,' it's Jane. She's not our mother, you know."

"I've got a mother," Andy snapped. "I also have a lot of teachers to lecture me so *you* needn't bother. I guess what I need is a friend." She banged out of the room without looking back.

Toby stared after her a moment, running her fingers down the sore muscles in her right arm. "I sure hit her on the wrong button! She may need a friend," she told the empty room, "but I need a forehand drive. Yet if that Gigi Norton can keep hitting those balls back, I can, too." She sighed and arched her tingling back. "I just have to work at it harder."

Toby thought about tennis all day. When she saw the grade on her geometry test she groaned, and promised herself she would make sure her homework was perfect to make up for it. She had only finished the first three problems before the sun, streaming across her desk in study hall, was too tempting. The first chance she had, she slipped out to go hit balls at the backboard. She went through the motions of going to all the rest of her classes, but couldn't keep her mind on what was going on. She groaned to find all the courts full after school, but she stood watching the players, instead of going back to the library to study. That night she bolted her supper and excused herself before anyone else had really started eating.

Andy stared after her. "How can she swallow this awful food that fast?"

"Maybe she's made a breakthrough," Maggie suggested, poking at an exhausted-looking dark mass on her plate. Her curly hair fell over her cheeks. "If she has figured out how to swallow this stuff without tasting it, she may end up rich and famous. What do you suppose this was before someone tortured it?"

Dee shook her head. "Spinach. But I don't think it was tortured. Mrs. Merriweather just dyed it black to go with those drowned orange carrots. After all, Halloween *is* only a few weeks away."

"If that's the case, it would be rude of us to eat it. I'm going to leave mine to decorate our plates tomorrow," Maggie said.

"And tomorrow, and tomorrow," Jane added, concentrating on the watery mashed potatoes.

"I wish I had caught Toby," Dee said. "I wanted to know what she's going to do with the English assignment we got today. It's scary to have one paper count as a fourth of your total grade. Where did she fly off to, anyway?"

"She has a tennis lesson down at the recreation center in the village," Jane told her. "It's an obsession with her. She's determined to lasso that game or turn in her spurs."

Maggie giggled. "Listen to who's talking Texas."

"I'm only quoting," Jane admitted.

"She should stick to her six-shooters," Dee said. "She can already outride anybody I ever saw. Tennis is only about seven thousand times harder than it looks."

Andy rose and started to empty her tray. "Wait and I'll walk up with you," Jane said.

Andy said nothing but waited. They walked upstairs together in an uncomfortable silence. Once inside the room, Jane turned to her. "I just wanted to apologize, Andy. I wasn't very sensitive this morning. But I really had a lot on my mind."

Andy shrugged and said hesitantly, "So did I."

Jane tightened her lips. "Andy, I am trying to apologize."

"And I'm just trying to tell you apologizing doesn't immediately make up for being . . . selfish. I want you to *act* as if you care about my problems!"

"Like you care about mine, I guess," Jane said slowly.

"How can I care about your problems when you make them for yourself?" Andrea stared at Jane without moving.

"There you go," Jane said. "Do you think anyone is this miserable on purpose? You've all just decided I'm rotten. Nobody even tries to see it from my point of view."

Andy glanced at her watch. "I have fifteen minutes before I have to face this awful final audition. I'd like something to take my mind off it for half an hour. Try me. Again."

Jane sat frowning a long moment. "First you have to understand about Neal and me. Our families have known each other forever.

And since Neal and I were just kids, our folks—"

"Your folks?" Andy asked quietly. "Are we talking about *your* problem or your parents'?"

"They're all mixed up together," Jane said.

Andy shook her head. "That's not right, Jane. What is important is between you and Neal."

Jane sighed. "You're right, of course. But I'm afraid Neal really might . . . well, think he loves me. That makes it worse."

"It does make it worse," Andy agreed. "Listen, Jane. I have a big brother. I've seen him fall in love and get hurt. But getting hurt is like cutting your finger; once it's over, you can start to heal. If you think Neal loves you and if you don't love him, you're hurting him more."

Jane began to cry without warning. Andy had never seen anyone cry the way Jane did. She didn't bawl or sob, she only laid those perfectly manicured white hands on her face and wept silently, with tears falling straight down to make darkened spots on the pale blue of her Oxford cloth shirt.

Andy wanted to put her arms around Jane and hold her close, but the memory of their sharp words earlier held her back.

"But what if his parents read the letter?" her voice muffled with tears.

"Write him," Andy said. "Be gentle. Phones don't work because of the shock. Neal needs your words on paper so he can read them over and over until they make sense to him."

"But what if his parents read the letter?" Jane asked, looking up.

Andy only held her eyes until Jane nodded. "I know. That's their problem, not Neal's and mine."

"I have only one question," Andy added. As she spoke, Maggie appeared in the doorway, practically exploding with happiness.

"Guess what wonderful thing!" Maggie cried. "You remember Faith, Jane. Her photographs have been chosen to be shown at a special exhibition in Boston in a couple of weeks. Her school is paying for the artists to come to Boston for an exhibit of their work. Wait until my sister hears. Dana will explode with pride! And if Faith has a chance, she's coming up to Canby Hall while she's here!" Maggie's voice trailed off as she looked from Andy to Jane and back. "Hey, did I barge in on something?"

Jane smiled. "You did, but never mind. I hope we get to see Faith."

"I'm really sorry," Maggie said, taking a step backward. "It *is* time for us to leave for the audition, Andy."

"I'll get my coat," Andy said, rising.

"Maggie," Jane said quietly. "Do you mind waiting for Andy out in the hall? She'll be out in a minute."

"No problem," Maggie said, backing out as swiftly as she had barged in.

Jane reached for Andy's hand. "I want to hear that question," she told Andy.

"This isn't my business, I know," Andy said.

Jane nodded. "Your other question?"

Andy almost whispered the words. "Have you told Cary Slade about Neal?"

Jane dropped her eyes and shook her head.

"No comment," Andy said. "Now cross your fingers for me. I'm off to the wars."

CHAPTER FIVE

Jane listened to Andy's footsteps fade along the wall, and looked for her stationery. It wasn't where she thought it was, but then, hardly anything ever was anymore. She sighed, and started looking again. Back home in Boston, everything was always where it belonged. Sarah, who had kept house for the Barrett family ever since Jane could remember, had as great a genius for picking things up and putting them away as Jane had for misplacing them.

When she finally found the box of stationery, at the bottom of her closet, she stared at it in horror. The problem was not with the stationery; it couldn't have been prettier. The paper was a rich cream color with her name engraved in her favorite color, Wedgwood blue. The envelopes were lined with the same color. The problem was that the stationery had been a birthday gift from Neal the year before.

"One does not write a things-aren't-what-you-think letter on his gift stationery," she told herself miserably. The *real* problem was that writing what she had to write gave her a hard pain in the pit of her stomach.

After making a dozen false starts, Jane groaned. A half hour had passed and she was no farther along than she had been when she started. She had homework to do. Maybe she should first rewrite the short story that was due in class the next day and *then* write Neal's letter.

Toby came in before her story was finished.

"How was tennis?" Jane asked, turning in her chair. She had to smile. Toby's red hair, which was always curlier than it needed to be, was a mass of springing damp ringlets around her face. With her cheeks flushed from exercise, her eyes were boldly, brilliantly green.

"Tennis," Toby said bluntly, "is the pits."

At Jane's astonished look, Toby fell across the bed, her legs hanging over the edge to drag on the floor. "That's not exactly accurate," Toby corrected herself. "I should have said that *I* am the pits at tennis."

"But you're still going to play?" Jane asked.

Toby glared at her. "You bet your life. A Houston doesn't run up a white flag for a stupid three-inch ball full of hot air!" She leaned over and pulled her towels from the rack by her dresser. "This will be my third shower today. I guess that's what makes them call tennis a good clean sport."

Jane tilted her head, listening. "It's quiet next door. I thought maybe Dee might be in there. She said something at dinner about wanting to talk to you about an English assignment."

Toby made a face. "That's the last thing I want to think about right now. Off to the showers."

Jane looked after her thoughtfully, realizing she hadn't seen Toby open a book for the past two days. Mind your own business! she told herself, and pulled another sheet of plain white paper from the drawer.

"Dear Neal," she began.

"Flowers for Barrett," Dee called from the doorway. The fragrance of the package she was carrying filled the room, even with a hood of green paper still in place. "They were delivered just as I walked in," Dee explained. "I told Mrs. Betts at the front desk that I'd bring them up."

A cluster of girls had walked up the stairs behind Dee. Jane saw Gigi Norton staring into the room, as Dee set the flowers down. Dee was waiting for Jane to unwrap them, her smile full of anticipation. Jane had no choice, but she unfastened the paper with a sinking heart. A clear glass bowl was filled with rose-colored heather mixed with white baby's breath.

"Whoever picked those out has class!" Dee told her.

Jane nodded over the lump in her throat, lifting the card fastened to a Wedgwood blue ribbon.

The card just read "Neal."

Such a huge crowd had turned up for the first audition that Andy wasn't prepared for how few people filed in to fill the seats in the auditorium that second night. In contrast to the noise and confusion before, the huge room was very quiet. Only a few chairs were filled and the people in them spoke to each other in quiet whispers. When the director came in, he walked down in front of the footlights and looked at them, one at a time, carefully.

"Several of you have asked me what production we are planning to work on," he said. "Many have asked me why the show's name wasn't announced on the earlier bulletins. This wasn't an oversight. Simply stated, this year's show is very special.

"This opera ballet has never been presented before." He smiled. "Given the importance of this event, we might even have Boston critics in our audience on opening night. The lyrics and score were written by Dario Raphael, who graduated from Oakley Prep several years ago and has gone on to achieve great fame as a composer in his native

Italy. The choreography was done by a friend
of Mr. Raphael's, who is equally noted in
Europe. Although the score is new, you all
know the story from your childhood. The title
is *The Sleeping Beauty.*

Andy felt her breath quicken. If critics
came from Boston, the dancers could get written up, or shown on tv. All her dreams of
being accepted by a major ballet school, of
working toward a lifetime of dancing, seemed
suddenly possible, as the director went on to
talk about the major scenes of the production.
His actual words spun past her, leaving im-
pressions rather than sense. She could see the
blaze of color as the ladies of the court crossed
and recrossed the stage. She saw the castle
with great stone rooms; the deep green of the
forbidding woods where the enchanted princess would lie. The prince and his hunter
companions. And of course, the dreaming
princess, rising gracefully from her bed.

Beside her, Maggie had clasped her hands
tightly together. Andy knew Maggie was seeing the sets, too, the turrets of the castle, the
green of forest trees, and was as excited as
Andy was.

The director's tone turned brisk. "Now to
the final casting," he said. "Tonight our work
really begins."

After a brief description of the routines he
wanted to see, he sent all the girl dancers
up onto the stage.

When the delicate melody of the piano

began, Andy felt herself floating. She recognized this feeling. When her lungs were filled with more air than she could breathe, her body would obey her every command. As she moved and swayed and leaped to the wonderful music, she felt she could almost burst with happiness.

When at last the music stopped, the line of dancers swept to the floor in deep formal bows. A patter of unexpected applause sounded from the audience.

"They *are* good, aren't they?" the director asked in a tone of delight, turning to the audience. "Very well, girls dismissed. Boys on stage."

He nodded with approval when the boys finished and sent them back to sit down.

"I would like to see the following dancers on stage," he announced, studying the notes in his hand. "Bailey, Kemperer, Frazier, Wong, MacDonald, Galloway, England. . . ."

Andy couldn't breathe. Her hands turned to ice as she clasped them in her lap, listening so hard that it hurt. ". . . And Cord."

Andy felt her heart stop as he spoke her name. Maggie caught her arm and squeezed it hard as Andrea rose to mount the stairs like a wooden puppet. The director described a new routine, repeated it carefully, and motioned for the house lights to be doused, leaving the stage brilliantly flooded.

Andy danced out from the wing, spun into the circle of light, and caught the arm of the boy who had approached from the other side of the stage. He was not much taller that she, but wonderfully strong. When the routine called for a lift, he spun her over his head with such grace that a patter of applause came from the darkness.

Only after they had been dismissed and Andy was sitting by Maggie, still panting a little to regain her breath, did she realize what had just happened. The names the director had read had been of the students picked for the *chorus*. She had lost the leading role to someone else and along with it the chance of her lifetime, thus far.

"Now that we have seen the chorus of ladies and gentlemen, let us see the prince and Sleeping Beauty. Will Ariadne Prentice and Mark Turner please come to the stage?"

Andy sat frozen. She had failed. Just when she had been so sure of herself in that first group dance, when everything had seemed to work right, she had failed. She had noticed the girl who was mounting the stage to a round of clapping. She was not very tall but walked with an immense dignity. Her hair was paler than Dee's and she had wound it up on her head in a great wreath of shining braids.

Andy hated her.

"She's a senior," Maggie whispered. "She was wonderful in the show last year."

Andy made herself nod as the music began. Not until that moment had she thought to

look around at the others who had been
chosen to be the chorus of ladies and gentlemen. They were all white, every one of them
except for a Chinese girl who was in Andrea's
geometry class. She looked at her rapt face
watching Ari Prentice and Mark Turner
dance. Was the girl figuring this out the same
way she was? Had it dawned on her that
neither of them had been chosen for the lead
because the lack of prejudice Canby Hall *said*
it was so big on was just a myth?

Andy used all the self-control she had to
hold back her tears. Her body was no problem, but she couldn't tighten muscles in her
mind to make it stay still. She watched the
couple dance with narrowed eyes. All right,
they were good. But they were no better than
some of the others. But they *were* white. Even
Mark Turner had pale hair and a fair skin
under the changing stage lights. How could
such a prince be given a black sleeping beauty
to waken?

How could she have kidded herself that
they would be fair about it? How was she
going to be able to tell her father what had
happened, that this famous old girl's school
which was supposed to have no ethnic bar-
riers at all was like the rest of the world when
it came to race?

She was grateful that the darkness hid her
disappointment and anger. She could leave.
In that darkness she could get up and leave
and forget the whole thing. "I decided I didn't

want to dance," she could tell her father.

He knew her too well. He would know there had to be a better reason why.

Maggie's hand was on her arm. "I'm so thrilled for you, Andy," she whispered. "It's just wonderful. I had no idea that the cast would be so small. Last year there was a giant chorus."

Andrea nodded, watching the finale of the dance. When Mark Turner raised Ari Prentice over his head, she seemed to float there. When she touched the floor, their joined rhythm was flawless.

For Andrea, to clap when the thunder of applause began was the same as telling a lie. But not to clap was to expose herself as a rotten sport to Maggie.

She clapped. Then the lights came on and Andy had to stand and smile at the dancers who had been disqualified, but had grace enough to come congratulate her.

Maggie knew a lot more of the girls than Andy did. The chatter went on and on, with Andy's control melting away by the minute. Finally she plucked at Maggie's sleeve and said, "I'm going on home alone."

Maggie started to protest but Andy didn't wait.

The chill night air stung on the tears that spilled down her cheeks the moment she was outside and alone.

Never mind how good you are, she thought. What color you are is more important.

CHAPTER SIX

Neither Toby nor Jane was prepared for the change in Andy after the audition. After their initial problems had been worked through, both girls had relaxed into the easy enjoyment of their three-way friendship. And in some ways, Andy had been the brightest spot in that friendship. Her warm, outgoing personality had been like sunshine in their crowded room.

But suddenly Andy's warmth was gone, leaving an astonishing sensitivity in its place. There was nothing too small for her to be touchy about. She barely talked at all but when she did, she was brief and cool and removed.

Neal continued to keep the flower deliveries coming for Jane after she refused his second invitation to Boston. When Andy came in and found a pot of blooming yellow tulips on her desk, she set them down on the floor with a thump.

"I'd appreciate your respecting my space," she said to Jane.

"I'm sorry," Jane said. "I thought you might enjoy them and there wasn't any room left anywhere else." That was true enough. In the space of a week, Neal had sent two bunches of cut flowers as well as the potted tulips.

"You could stop all that nonsense with a postage stamp," Andy said. "Or is honesty too painful?"

Jane winced. Honesty *was* painful. But so was trying to talk to Andy. "I wrote the letter," she said quietly.

Andy's dark eyes were questioning. "Did you mail it?"

"I mailed the letter," Jane said coldly, fighting her annoyance. Okay, so she had carried the letter around for several days before dropping it in the Baker House mail slot, which was famous for irregular pickups.

Fortunately Andy let it drop and turned back to her geometry book. Jane studied her on the sly. Even Andy's beauty had changed. Instead of glowing vitality, Andy's face seemed frozen. She looked more like a shadowy statue than a warm, feeling girl.

But Toby wasn't the same, either. She had always complained about her homework and put it off to the last moment, but in the end she did it well and on time. Since taking up tennis, she didn't mention her schoolwork at all, and got annoyed when anyone else did.

The one time Jane mentioned that she never saw Toby open a book anymore, Toby glared at her. "That's between me and my teachers, isn't it?"

But a week of Andy's moodiness annoyed Toby as much as the subject of her schoolwork. With her customary bluntness, she challenged Andy on the way she was acting. "Hey," she said. "I don't get all this. It's not as if you had washed out of the play, like most of the kids did. You have a part, and a good one. Maggie says —"

"Maggie should learn not to talk about other people's business," Andy said.

Toby's cheeks flamed with color. "It may not be any of Maggie's business, but it sure is my business and Jane's. We have to live with you."

"Well," Andy said, "somebody has to make the sacrifice if Baker House is to have its show-and-tell black girl."

Toby whistled softly as Andy went out of the room, her head held high.

"So that's what's eating her!" She turned to Jane. "Got any ideas on how we can get that chip off her shoulder?"

Jane shook her head. "I'm afraid to say anything to her for fear she may bite my head off."

"Do you suppose she really thinks she is in this room and only in the chorus just because she's black?" Toby asked with a sudden frown. "And is she right? Could she have been the

best dancer and lost the starring role because
that other girl is a senior and white?"

"No," Maggie said firmly from the doorway. "Sorry to barge in like this, but that's
the penalty of having Dee and me next door.
I forget and just pop in without being asked.
But the play was honestly cast. Ari *is* better
for the part. She can't dance that much better
than Andy but she has more stage presence.
Maybe it's because she's been in so many more
performances. Andy's picked the wrong reason for not getting the star role."

"She wouldn't be acting like this if she
didn't really believe it. Somebody she respects should talk to her about it," Jane said.

"I wish Faith Thompson were here," Maggie said. "Andy might listen to another black
girl on the subject of Canby Hall."

"But Faith isn't here," Jane said. She
paused. "Andrea likes and respects Alison
Cavanaugh. Maybe we should talk to her."

Toby grinned. "When in doubt, dump on
our housemother?" Naturally, Andy liked and
respected Alison. Who could help it? If it
hadn't been for Alison, the house mother for
Baker House, the three of them would never
have begun being friends.

Alison was not only fun to look at, she was
just the kind of woman Toby hoped to be
some day. Alison was very slender and even
taller than Toby but every move she made
was graceful. Her wavy brown hair shone and
her eyes under large, horn-rimmed glasses,

danced. The apartment where she lived with
her cat Doby was the only living space on the
top floor and the most inviting room Toby
had ever seen. There were three comfortable
armchairs and bright pillows everywhere.
The room held lots of plants and pictures and
posters, and a coffee table covered with maga-
zines.

She frowned, hating to bother Alison so
soon with another problem from Room 407.
"Let's give Andy some more time. Neither of
us is at her best right now, either. This tennis
business is driving me bonkers, and you're
going to be edgy until you stop this flower
shower from Whoever The Third, who obviously has more money than brains."

Jane laughed. "His name is Cornelius
Worthington III, and he really has brains
enough. But you may be right about Alison."
If they needed her, Alison would be there.
Jane really didn't see Alison that often but
just knowing that she was up there was com-
forting. And Toby had a good point. Maybe
Andy just needed more time.

Toby left the room with her tennis bag over
her shoulder to catch an hour of practice before dark. In spite of a daily lesson and practicing on the backboard at least twice a day,
she could see little improvement in her game.
The coach at the recreation department had
begun bragging about her "spectacular improvement," but Toby sure couldn't see it.

She kept forgetting to keep her elbow close to her body and her follow-through was just rotten. She had even bought a second racket and went back and forth between them, unable to decide which one she played the best with.

Finding all the courts empty, Toby set down her bag of balls and began practicing her serve. She had gone through the bag twice before moving over to the backboard. She was too engrossed in trying to see how many returns she could make to realize that a bunch of girls had stopped outside the fence.

She glanced over. The only one she recognized was Gigi Norton.

"Don't stop for us!" Gigi called. Her voice was light with amusement. "We love your Texas comedy routine on how *not* to play tennis." At her words, the little group of girls rippled with laughter before moving on.

Toby picked up a ball and slammed it against the backboard, wishing the silly thing would split wide open.

She hated Gigi Norton. She hated this ridiculous game and the way she played it. She hated the way her grades were falling. But she couldn't do everything at once. Winter was coming and she wouldn't be able to use the outside court at all. *Then* she would catch up on her back work. *Then* she would tackle that crazy English assignment that Dee was spending hours in the library working on.

She also hated that she was doing all this

for Randy Crowell and she hadn't even seen
him since she began this whole stupid tennis
business. She hated the way things in Room
407 were, with Andy marching around spoil-
ing for a fight and Jane agonizing over
whether to be honest or not with her collection of men.

Most of all, she hated being away from her
dad and her home. At the thought of them,
she felt instant tears fill her eyes. Back at the
ranch her dad would be readying for the
roundup. The ranchers always set the fall
roundup by the Farmer's Almanac. The way
the phase of the moon fell, the roundup was
usually the last three days before her birthday. She always got excused from school to
spend that time in the saddle, working beside
her dad.

The spring roundup in April was fun but
the fall roundup was wonderful and sad all
at once. The spring and summer calves, sepa-
rated from their mothers for the first time,
bawled all night and would have kept her
awake if she hadn't been so worn out from
riding and roping.

The big party at the end of the round-up
was always called "October's Birthday Blast"
because of her birthday. Her cake had to be
big enough to serve thirty people with second
helpings. Someone usually brought big con-
tainers of ice cream packed in rock salt and
ice. The meat was cooked outside over mes-
quite all afternoon with the smell of tomato

sauce and spices filling the air. After everybody was too full to stand up, the cowboys
sang around the fire until the harvest moon
was halfway across the sky.

Toby was grateful for the falling darkness
as she dragged back toward Baker House. She
wanted to bawl like a calf herself, when she
saw the moon rising over Sycamore Grove on
its way toward Texas.

CHAPTER
SEVEN

Andy was still away when Toby got back to the room. An open box of brownies lay on her desk where Jane had set the tulips.

"Don't tell me Andy got more food from home?" Toby asked Jane.

Jane nodded. "You remember those brownies. Andy's mom brought some when her family came here to visit her. She calls them Jo's Folly."

Toby frowned, sliding out of her warm-up suit. "That's a funny name for a cookie."

Jane smiled. "Mrs. Cord got the recipe from somebody named Jo. She insists every square has seven thousand calories, which certainly makes every one you eat pure folly. Andy put them out for anyone who wants them."

"Where is Andy?"

Jane shrugged. "I didn't ask her."

Her tone was so bleak that Toby frowned at her. "I'm on my way to the village for tennis right after dinner. Isn't Cary working in the diner tonight? You could spend an hour there with him and we'd walk back together. You know that Alison likes us to only go out at night in twos."

Jane frowned, glancing at her desk. "I haven't finished my homework. I really ought to stay in and do it." It was on the tip of her tongue to ask Toby when she was going to study, but she held it back. She didn't want her head taken off by Toby, either.

"We won't be late getting back," Toby told her.

Jane nodded, really tempted. Then she shook her head. "I'd love to go but we haven't a date."

"Hey," Toby protested. "You don't have to have a date to drop in for a Coke where your friend works." Then she laughed. "Listen to who's telling you how to run your social life! I've never had a boyfriend in my life."

Jane rose, smiling. "See how easy it was to talk me into that? I'll walk to the village with you."

They signed out on the sheet on their door and left.

Jane dropped Toby at the Greenleaf Recreational Building. "I'll come by the diner for you when I get through," Toby said. "Wish me luck with my fine collection of thumbs."

Jane hesitated outside the diner. She had never gone in alone like this when Cary was on duty. Was this something a well-bred lady shouldn't do? Then she put it to the final test. Would her older sister Charlotte do this? She had never gone wrong by asking her sister's advice about things like this. But with Charlotte off at Smith College, she was harder to reach. Anyway, this was silly. She should be able to make up her own mind about her own boyfriend! She drew a deep breath, pretended she was Charlotte, and pushed the door open.

Jane knew she had done the right thing when Cary looked up from the back of the diner and smiled broadly at her. He was at her side in a minute.

"Hey, surprise! Fabulous!" he said. "You want a booth?" He hesitated. "On second thought, if you sit here at the counter I can talk to you between orders."

"The counter is fine," she said, sliding onto the nearest stool.

He was around in back of the counter in a flash, looking very professional and eager. "Now, madam, what is your pleasure? We feature an international cuisine here . . . German chocolate cake, French silk pie, Italian lasagna, Polish sausage?"

Jane laughed. "I'll have them all," she said flippantly. "With lots of whipped cream but hold the nuts."

He nodded and reached for the tongs to pull a massive steaming sausage from the broiler. "No!" she cried. "I was only kidding. Hot chocolate will be fine."

"I'll hold the nuts." He nodded.

A bus came into the adjoining station, bringing a rush of business, but within a few minutes everyone's order had been taken and she and Cary could talk again. It was fun just to watch Cary, to study the line of his head and the way he moved, sometimes carrying an astonishing number of dishes and plates. After that, customers came in one or two at a time. Jane was fascinated watching him win strangers over. Sometimes customers stared at his long hair and that single earring gleaming above his open-necked shirt and looked doubtful. Usually they relaxed the minute he smiled and asked for their orders.

It was funny about Cary. As much as she loved it when he smiled, she loved seeing his face sober. His expressions turned almost brooding, sad, and somehow romantic.

In between customers, and when he had the tables cleared and wiped off, he leaned on the counter by her and talked about the coming Harvest Moon Dance at Oakley Prep. "I can't wait for you to hear the new sound the Ambulance has put together," he told Jane. "I wish I could describe it. It's still rock but it's a departure." He nodded. "A real departure, the kind of sound you don't want to have stop."

Jane listened, wondering if he could tell that she felt the same way about hearing him talk. She knew she could sit there forever and just listen to him. But then, she felt the same

way when he was playing his guitar. He caught
her eyes on his and smiled, leaning toward
her. "I don't think there's another girl on
earth who can listen like you can," he said
gently.

"Maybe they don't have anyone as nice as
you talking to them," she said, then blushed
at her own words.

Golden moment.

The door banged open, bringing in a fresh
wave of cold air. The compact room seemed
to shrink from the noisy chatter of the bunch
of girls who raced each other to a booth, tugging off their jackets and laughing at each
other.

Before Cary even got glasses of water filled
to take to them, Jane realized that Gigi Norton was in the group. She breathed in carefully. Having to room with Gigi her first
year at Canby Hall had been one of the worst
experiences of her life. Just the sound of
Gigi's voice, always too loud, made her cringe.

"Well, look who's here!" Gigi said loudly.
"Hi, Jane."

When Jane turned on the stool to reply,
Gigi went on. "Three guesses why you're here.
I bet you left Baker for the same reason we
did." She smiled up at Cary as he set down
her glass of water. "We're going to report
Jane to the environmental authorities. Some
boy friend of hers has taken to sending her
flowers every ten minutes. The entire fourth
floor of Baker smells like a funeral parlor.

We complain, of course, but at heart we're all *very* jealous. It must be nice, Barrett!"

Cary turned and met her eyes. His look of surprise made her cringe. Jane looked back, begging him to wait, not to react to Gigi until she could explain.

Instead, he held her eyes a long minute, the surprise being replaced by anger before he turned away. Gigi covered her mouth with her hand, her eyes narrowing. "Oh my goodness! Don't tell me I told tales out of school. What a loudmouth I am."

"Do you have your orders ready?" Cary asked, interrupting Gigi and staring hard at her with those intense dark eyes. During the flurry of their conversations as they opened their menus, Jane sat very still, waiting. Cary would let her explain. She only had to force herself to wait until he had free time.

When Cary had placed their orders in the kitchen and delivered their drinks to the table, he came back to stand in front of Jane.

"It *must* be nice." He quoted Gigi, his voice low and angry. "I can't believe you're getting some big rush and not even mentioning it. Who is this guy, anyway? What's going on between you and him?"

Jane leaned toward him. "I meant to tell you, Cary, I really did. I just haven't had a chance."

"No chance? We've been talking here for almost an hour. You had a million chances."

"It's not that easy, Cary," Jane pleaded.

The booth filled with the girls was very quiet, as Gigi and her friends shamelessly tried to overhear her conversation with Cary. "It's Neal back in Boston. We've been friends a long time. You remember, you met him once right here in the diner."

He interrupted. "I remember you said he was an old friend, but you didn't mention he was a flower-sending old friend. Have you told him you're dating me?"

Jane felt herself flush. "I haven't had a chance to."

He wiped angrily at the counter in front of her. "No chance, no chance," he said angrily. "I don't get this at all, Jane, but what I get I don't like. Why the flowers; what's his big pitch?"

"Cary," she pleaded. "Can't we talk about this some other time . . . like when we don't have an audience?"

He studied her, his eyes cold. "How about when you've told this other fish on your string about me?"

As he spoke the bell rang at the little window in the kitchen, signaling him that the girls' orders were ready.

"Cary . . ." she begged. But he had turned and walked away from her. As he did, Toby opened the door and stuck her head in.

Jane was off her stool reaching for her coat in one swift movement. She stood by the cash register a minute, waiting for Cary to be through and come back. Then she turned to

Toby. "I didn't even ask you if you wanted a drink or something to eat?" she said.

Before Toby could reply, Cary was there. "Ninety-five cents," he told Jane without meeting her eyes.

She fished out the coins and laid them down. "Cary," she began.

"Tell me when you're *really* ready to talk," he said, his eyes hostile on hers.

Toby, her red curls damp around her face, studied him a moment, then looked back at the noisy booth that held Gigi and her crowd. She turned and opened the door for Jane.

"Good-night, Cary," she said quietly.

What he mumbled was less than a greeting. His parting glance at Jane made her want to die.

CHAPTER EIGHT

The practice schedule for the musical was posted on the bulletin board when Maggie and Andy got to the auditorium that Monday evening. Maggie whistled softly as they looked for their names on the sheet. Because Maggie was listed as a prompter, she only had to report when lines were being practiced. Andy had twice as many scheduled hours, because there were also special practice sessions for the dances.

"You are going to be busy!" Maggie said.

"There's not much else to do around here," Andy said, shrugging.

"Well, there's always studying," Maggie reminded her. "Midterm grades come this week."

"Some people manage to get along without studying at all," Andy said. "My roommate, for instance."

It was on the tip of Maggie's tongue to ask which of her roommates she meant. The state-

ment could apply to either Toby or Jane.
Toby had become a missing person up on the
fourth floor. She was either on her way to
practice tennis, coming in from practicing, or
standing in a hot shower groaning from sore
muscles.

Jane was a different case. She was there in
body, but absent in mind. She sat at her desk
with an open notebook, or curled in bed with
a book, but it was all sham. If you asked her
a question, her mind had to be pulled back
from somewhere far away. Room 407 was
not the room it had been.

"Well, at least Toby's efforts at tennis are
paying off," Maggie said. "Dee says she is
really getting good."

Andy bit her lip. "For some people just
being good is enough."

Maggie refused to pick up on Andy's remark, not knowing how to answer.

Maggie was among the first of the backstage
crew to arrive. She stood in the shadow of the
curtain looking out into the auditorium. The
room held many memories for her.

She remembered coming down from New
York City with her mom to hear her sister
Dana sing in the chorus. How long ago that
seemed, before her father's remarriage and
his move to Hawaii. Maggie was glad Dana
had decided to spend this year in Hawaii with
their dad and his wife and new baby, instead
of starting college. Maggie herself would never
have accepted her dad's marriage as a good

thing if she hadn't spent the summer with him and his new family.

And Shelley! How could Maggie stand on this stage and forget the fabulous job Shelley Hyde had done in the senior play? Even Maggie's mother, who was used to seeing sophisticated New York productions, was impressed. "I can't believe our Shelley has blossomed from a little Iowa country girl into such a beautiful and talented actress in just these few years!" And Shelley really had. Maggie was convinced Shelley would have made it as an actress in New York, if she hadn't decided to go back to the University of Iowa and study drama there.

Faith was the only one who was living close to Canby Hall, if you could call Rochester, New York, close. But Faith had had to borrow money to pad out her scholarship. It wasn't likely she could afford anything as frivolous as just coming back to visit Canby Hall for pleasure. This photography exhibit made a difference.

Maggie hated seeing anyone as unhappy as her friends in 407 were; each in her own way. Dana and Faith and Shelley had had their differences, too. But in the end they had worked everything out. Maybe Jane and Andrea and Toby would, too.

Maggie had disappeared behind the curtain before the dancers were called up on stage. In spite of her resentment, Andy had become really caught up in the routine. In the court scenes the lines of dancers flowed back and forth like moving water. If the director would just quit yelling at her all the time, she was sure that the practices would just be heaven.

The music began, breaking into her thoughts. She was just relaxing into it when he barked at her *again*.

"One, two, three, four," he chanted. "Pick it up, there. Lively on the turn. Five, six, seven, eight. Very nice. All except Cord. Smile!"

Andy forced her head up and tried to smile. She was going to count how many times an evening he singled her out like that. It was always the same. "All except Cord. Smile, Andrea . . . smile!"

"I could always quit," she told herself. "I could quit and let them find some Cheshire cat to smile in my place." But she knew she wouldn't. After the first few minutes, she could forget him, and the injustice of the casting, and just come alive in the dance. When she finished her closing solo, she was surprised by a patter of applause from high up in the darkness beyond the footlights. The director heard it, too, because she saw him look around. Then, amazingly, he nodded at her approvingly. "Very good, Cord," he told her. "But smile!"

Toby didn't even stop at the desk in the lobby on her way in from tennis. She never got messages, anyway, and only got mail on Thursdays when her dad's Sunday letter arrived. She nodded at Mrs. Betts and was starting upstairs when the desk attendant called her back.

"Just a minute, Toby. You have a slip in your box."

A crazy surge thumped in Toby's chest. She hadn't been out to Randy's ranch since the day she decided to take up tennis. Maybe he had missed her. Maybe he had called.

Mrs. Betts smiled as she handed Toby the folded note. "Have a nice evening, honey."

Toby smiled and nodded, too eager to read the message to think of a response. She waited until she was in the light of the landing to open it. The printed form letter had Alison Cavanaugh's signature at the bottom. Alison wanted to see her. Toby glanced at her watch. "Between seven-thirty and nine o'clock on Monday." It was eight forty-five. Toby whistled softly. Getting clear up to Alison's apartment on the top floor on time meant running straight up there, dirty sweats and all. She couldn't even stop in 407 to drop off her tennis gear.

Toby was breathless by the time she reached the hall outside Alison's door. She could hear the rhythm of Alison's stereo. Stopping, she tugged at her clothes and shoved at her hair, which was still damp from tennis. Alison opened the door at her knock and stepped back for her to come in.

"Good! You did make it," Alison said, smiling. "I checked with Mrs. Betts when it started getting late. I haven't been watching the sign-out sheet that closely. Do you go for tennis every evening?"

"I have so far," Toby said, standing uncertainly inside the door. Doby leaped from his cushion to approach her, purring loudly.

"Am I ever rude!" Alison rebuked herself. "Have a cushion. Tea or Coke?"

Toby hesitated. "Tea if it's not too much trouble."

Alison smiled. "Hot water is hot water in this world of tea bags." She set a box of assorted cookies on the table as she spoke.

Doby jumped up beside Toby and pressed his warm body tight against her leg. Toby nibbled at a sandwich cookie until Alison returned with two mugs of tea and sat down across from her.

"I'll get right into why I called you here," Alison said brightly. "I'm sure you remember Miss Allardyce's speech about our new computer?" At Toby's nod, she went on. "That is one very clever machine. Maybe too clever. It not only matches up roommates, it keeps class records and grade scores current on a day-to-day basis."

Toby concentrated on her tea, suddenly scared of what might be coming.

"To get to the point, our electronic wizard isn't reporting very good news about you." She laid a sheet of printed, punched paper on the table. "October Houston," she read. "According to the printout, you've been late to your geometry class ten times in the last ten days. It also reports that you've left study hall early seven of those days, and missed every library night you were assigned to."

Alison paused and looked up at Toby. After a long moment of silence, she added, "No comment?"

"I've been working at my tennis game."

Alison nodded. "But not studying."

Toby shrugged. "I can catch up when I can't practice outside anymore."

Alison shook her head. "That's not the way learning works, Toby. You stack what you learn one day on what you learned yesterday, like bricks. I hate to come down on you like this when you're just settling in. I know boarding school is a big adjustment, but it *is* a school. Nothing is as important in the long run as what you carry away from here in your head. Even if your grades were all right, Canby Hall has rules that have to be followed. And your grades so far are not acceptable."

Toby looked up, startled. "You don't mean they are going to kick me out?"

Alison's expression was very sober. "The rules are designed to give you every possible chance. Sending you home without any warning wouldn't be fair. But the academic standards at Canby Hall were set before either of us were born. It's my responsibility to give you a first warning and tell you that if your grades don't come up in the next three weeks, you'll have to explain it to Miss Allardyce. If they aren't up by semester end, there may be some question of whether you can come back. Now, I've done my duty in warning you. Let's talk about how I can help you straighten this out."

Toby shook her head. "I don't need any help. I got myself into this mess, I'll have to get myself out. I'll try to do better, I really will."

"Perhaps you could start by cutting the tennis lessons down to one or two a week."

Toby looked at her aghast. "But I'm only just beginning to make progress."

"In tennis," Alison reminded her. "This is a school, Toby, not an athletic camp. You're here to learn, not play games." She smiled as if to soften her words. "Now a game can't be *that* important, can it?"

Toby looked down at her hands. The right one was calloused from gripping her racket. Alison would never understand how important it was for her to play tennis well enough to impress Randy. She wouldn't understand how it was to get this old and never have a boy you liked.

"Can it?" Alison asked again.

"I guess not," Toby admitted.

Alison's smile was as warm as her hand on Toby's. "You'll make a real effort, then?"

Toby nodded and rose, stirring Doby from

her side. "A real effort," she echoed, knowing in her heart that she was only going to make what effort she could in the time she had left over from tennis.

Toby walked downstairs slowly. She wished she had asked Alison if anyone was going to write home to her dad about her grades. She could see him back home at the round kitchen table, studying her elementary school grade cards line by line.

"English . . . A, history . . . A," and so on until he'd read all the way through. "Two things you got from your mom," he would say, grinning over at her. "Those carrot curls of yours and the brains under them. You make me proud, Toby, plumb proud."

But tennis weather was almost over. She could catch her grades up before semester's end, she knew she could.

The room was dead quiet when Toby entered. Andy was at her desk with her back to the door. She didn't even look around. Jane glanced up from her book with a distracted expression.

The phone rang, but no one answered it. When it rang the second time, Toby came alive and reached back for it.

"Baker House," she said absently.

The accent on the other end of the line brought her up sharply. That was a Boston accent, just like Jane's. The words were as formal as the clipped tone in which they were spoken. "This is Gloria Barrett and I'm calling from Boston. Could I speak to my daughter Jane, please?"

"Yes, sir, I mean yes, ma'am," Toby stammered. "Just a minute. I'll get her."

"It's your mom," Toby blurted out to her. "She's calling long distance."

Jane's eyes were suddenly terrified. "I could tell her you aren't here," Toby suggested in a whisper.

Jane shook her head. "After hours? Thanks, anyway, Toby."

Jane paused and crossed her fingers. Toby crossed her fingers on both hands just as if she knew why she was doing it.

CHAPTER NINE

Jane held her breath a moment before taking the receiver. "Mom?" she asked. "Toby said it was you." She could have kicked herself for the funny wavery way her voice sounded. "Is everything all right at home?"

"Everything is fine *here*," her mother said.

The silence that followed seemed very pointed. "You and Dad are fine, and Sarah?" Jane asked.

"*Everything* is fine here." Her mother's voice was firm. "Now that we have that behind us, why don't you tell me how things are *there*?"

Jane couldn't bring herself to mention Cary or Neal. "Just wonderful!" she said, hearing the falseness in her own voice. "Andy got a dancing part in the musical and Toby is getting to be a really good tennis player."

Silence hit again. "That's very nice, but I want to hear about you, Jane." The pause was brief. When her mother spoke again, Jane heard a familiar edge of irritation in her voice. "Now don't tell me about your classes or the awful things Mrs. Merriweather is expecting you to eat. I want some explanation about you and Neal. He is *very* upset."

"Did he talk to you?"

"Of course he talked to me, Jane. I've known that boy all his life. What's more, his mother talked to me . . . not just talked, but came to the house. I didn't see your letter, but I did hear about it. Neal *is* a gentleman, you know. But your father and I are completely unable to understand what impulse made you upset Neal like this. What do you think you are doing?"

"Mom." Jane struggled to find the words. "I'm not *doing* anything. I was just being honest with Neal, the way I've always been taught. I thought I owed it to him. . . ."

Her mother didn't let her finish. "You owe Neal more than some silly letter, telling him that you're interested in another boy. Of course, you are interested in other boys. I'm quite sure Neal sees attractive young ladies in whom he's interested, too, but does he write you about them?"

"Mom," Jane protested. "You don't understand. Neal asked me home twice. When I didn't accept the second time he got really angry on the phone. Then he started sending me flowers." Jane hated to quote that awful Gigi but the words slipped out. "This place smells like a funeral parlor."

"Jane." Her mother was plainly shocked. "That remark is in extremely poor taste. I can't believe you are behaving like this. It simply isn't like you. Your father and I have talked this over. We agree that you owe Neal an apology. You have hurt him deeply."

"I was only being honest," Jane said.

"Sometimes there is a thin line between honesty and pointless tactlessness." Her mother's tone softened. "My dear, you cannot disrupt a friendship of such long standing because of a girlish crush. The Barretts and Worthingtons have been friends for generations. Remember who Cornelius is. He's part of our lives. He's like us."

The rest of the conversation barely registered on Jane. Her mother not only didn't understand, she didn't even care about Jane's feelings. . . . Neal and his precious mother were all that mattered. When her mother finally said goodnight, Jane replaced the receiver and looked at the phone longingly. More than anything she needed to talk to her sister. Charlotte would have good advice. Charlotte always knew how to put things in a way their mother would accept. But could even Charlotte make her see clearly about Cornelius Worthington III?

Jane picked up her towels and robe and walked down the hall to the showers, leaving Andrea and Toby staring after her.

Maggie, looking like a leprechaun in her bright green ski pajamas, passed Jane on the way to the shower room. She paused, peering through her glasses with concern. "You okay, Jane?" she asked.

Jane forced herself to smile. "Parent trouble," she said.

Maggie shook her head dolefully. "Poor creatures! What would they do if they didn't have us to educate them?" Jane looked after her. What wonderful ideas that girl had! But how could anyone possibly teach her mother that Jane also had feelings that could be hurt as painfully as Neal Worthington's could be?

Toby, more concerned than she wanted to admit by Alison's warning, set her alarm extra early to be sure she could get a full hour on the court and still make it to her geometry class on time. Every morning seemed colder than the last. She could blow her breath in a cloud of steam and her knuckles were blue as she gripped the racket. She served a whole bag of balls. As she kicked the balls together to start over, she saw Dee approaching the fence.

"Boy, are you dedicated!" Dee said. "You're an inspiration. If I had my stuff with me, I'd hit a few balls with you."

Toby smiled. "You don't want to hit with a rank beginner."

"You may have started as a beginner, but you're mastering this game quicker than anyone I ever saw."

Toby went up to the fence. "How long have you been playing?"

Dee laughed. "Typical California kid. I guess I had my first group class at about six. I know I had to hold the racket up with both hands. Mom still has the blue ribbon I got for Most Improved."

"And you've played ever since?"

Dee nodded. "You've found out for yourself what a hold the game gets on you."

"You really like tennis *that* well?" Toby asked.

Dee stared at her. "Of course I do. You must, too, the way you've been obsessed by it this fall." As she spoke the chimes sounded the hour in the carillon. "Whoops, I got to hike or get a tardy mark."

"Me, too, I guess," Toby said, slinging her backpack of balls over her shoulder. "Alison had me on the carpet last night."

"For lateness?"

Toby nodded, a little embarrassed. "*And* missing study periods, *and* not turning up at the library, *and* letting my grades slip."

Dee whistled. "That sounds like the whole truck dumped on you! But you couldn't have been surprised."

"What do you mean by that?" Toby bridled.

"Come on." Dee laughed. "You came here to get a high school education. You've lived, eaten, and breathed tennis lately. Don't forget, I have classes with you. I bet you haven't even started on that English project yet. You had to expect this was coming."

Toby shook her head. "I figured I could

catch up when it got too cold for outdoor tennis." They walked along together.

Dee stopped in the path. "I'm having trouble getting this together, Toby. First you practically tell me that you're not really wild about this game, then you say you were willing to deliberately risk your grades for it. What's the deal?"

Dee's look was so direct that Toby felt herself flushing. She knew her face was as red as her hair as she dropped her eyes.

"Toby!" Dee said in disbelief. "Look at you blush. It's a guy. You're doing all this for some guy! I don't believe you."

"Well, he's not just *any* guy." Toby said hotly, angry at being so easy to see through.

"I don't care *who* he is," Dee said. "Any guy who doesn't like you just the way you are isn't going to like you any bettter for being kicked out of school. Where's your pride?" As she spoke, she marched up the stairs to her class with her back straight. "I'd like to see the guy I'd put myself that far out for."

"It's not like that at all," Toby protested. "It's just that . . . I wanted to have more in common with him."

Dee stopped dead and turned to look at her thoughtfully. "I just put two and two together, October Houston. The only time I've seen you with a guy is when you were riding horseback with Randy Crowell. Randy is a nice guy, but believe me, Toby, not even Randy Crowell is worth that! Any time you have to change your-self for a guy, he's the *wrong* guy."

Toby stared after Dee as she ran on up the stairs. She wanted to argue with Dee, to pro-test that she wasn't really changing herself, but first she would have to decide if that was the honest truth.

Mrs. Offutt didn't say anything sarcastic, but she lifted her eyebrows in mock astonish-ment when Toby slipped into her seat just before the bell rang. When papers started passing her, being handed toward the front of the room, Toby slid down in her seat. How could she have forgotten they had an assign-ment to turn in? The teacher riffled through the papers and looked at her.

"You have your choice of excuses, October. You either forgot to do the work or you forgot to bring it."

"I forgot to do it," Toby admitted.

The annoyed look changed to one of grudg-ing respect. "I give points for honesty. If you can get it in tomorrow, I will not take off late points." Toby stammered her thanks and opened her book, conscious that everyone in the room was looking at her.

For the first time since she started tennis, Toby went to the library instead of the court after school. She worked an hour on the assignment she had forgotten to do and couldn't get it to come out right. She could almost hear Alison's voice in her head. "You stack what you learn one day on what you learned yesterday, like bricks."

Okay, so she had to go back and put some bricks under that lesson to do it. She worked until the girl at the desk signaled that the library was closing for the dinner hour. By the time she got back to Baker House, everyone else had already gone to the dining room.

Toby didn't think she was hungry until she was inside the door. She sniffed the air in disbelief! Chili! The air smelled like chili, her favorite food. She set the tray down at the last open place at the table with Maggie Morrison.

"Wow!" she said, unfolding her napkin. "This smells great." At Maggie's lifted eyebrow, she laughed. "You don't like chili?"

"I *love* chili," Maggie said. "But I don't like tomato and bean soup with dead meat in it."

Toby lifted a spoonful, tasted it, then stared at Maggie. "What did she do to this?"

Maggie nodded. "I don't know whether it's something she did or something she didn't."

"But it *smells* right!" Toby protested.

"She does that with a spray can," Maggie told her, stacking her tray to leave.

Jane was the first one back in the room after dinner. By the time Andy came in and changed into her dancing clothes, Jane had put on a plush robe and tied her hair back with a ribbon. Her creative writing assignment was to write a scene showing a violent negative emotion. If the memory wasn't so painful, she would have tried to describe Cary's furious face at the diner.

Andy quietly left for rehearsal without interrupting Jane, and then Toby came in. At the rattle of coat hangers, Jane looked up to see Toby pulling her jacket out of the closet.

"I might as well have a single room as live with you and Andy," Jane told her. "But you'll need a scarf if you're going to walk to the village and back tonight. It's getting cold out there. Anyway, where are you going alone?"

"I'm just going to the library," Toby told her. "That's allowed."

"No tennis lesson?"

Toby shook her head. "Alison had me in for a stiff talk last night."

"Grades?" Jane asked. At Toby's nod, Jane sighed. "Anything I can do to help?"

Toby grinned. "I guess there is. If you see me picking up that racket, hit me with it. I'd sure like to be back home in Texas but I don't want to be *sent*."

With Toby gone, Jane stared at the clipboard and thought about Cary. For the first time since they'd connected, he hadn't called her in three whole days. Gigi and her big mouth. Jane glared at the fresh arrangement of white asters and blue iris that had been waiting at the desk when she got back to Baker. She wanted to pitch them out the window. Instead, she began to cry without meaning to. Tears she couldn't stop just started flowing silently down her face. She was rummaging in her desk looking for a tissue, when Dee Adams spoke from the door.

"Toby around?" she asked. Then, seeing Jane's face, she hesitated.

"At the library," Jane told her, having to sniffle before she spoke.

"Which of those guys are you crying for?" Dee asked. "You can't cry for yourself because you're in charge."

"Thanks for the lecture," Jane said hotly. "Now if you'll just excuse me. . . ." She looked away from Dee but was conscious of the girl standing in the doorway, studying her. As always, Jane was struck with the glow of relaxed confidence that was as much a part of Dee as her mane of blond hair and her rich tan. Tonight she had on an electric blue blouse, and it lit up the room.

When the phone rang Jane said, "Answer it, Dee. Please. If it's for me. . . ."

"Don't tell me, let me guess," Dee said. "You're not here, right?" She shook her head. "I don't lie for myself or anybody else, Jane. I'm sorry. The only games I play are on courts."

She was gone and the phone was still ringing. Jane, flushed with shame, walked over to it, and picked up the receiver.

Jane had always really liked Neal's mother. From her earliest memory, when the families

had spent holidays together at the Worthingtons' summer place on Cape Cod, Mrs. Worthington had been one of her favorite people.
Still, Jane felt her heart hit the bottom of her
stomach when she recognized Mrs. Worthington's voice.

"Jane, dear."

Neal's mother's words flowed like cream.
There was no reproach in her voice at all, only
some mild amusement. "Neal wanted to get
in touch with you himself but he's buried in
midterms. But I thought you should know,
dear, when he heard you weren't coming up
for his school dance, he decided not to go,
either. He said it just wouldn't be any fun
without you."

"I wish he wouldn't do that!" Jane protested.

"He's being very stubborn, isn't he?" Mrs.
Worthington went on smoothly. "But there's
no reasoning with him." She laughed softly.
"He simply misses you, that's all! He has decided to come visit you at Canby Hall this
weekend. I told him he *must not* get in the
way of your plans, and he promised he
wouldn't. He was going to call you himself,
but I told him I would, since I wanted to say
hello, anyway."

"Here?" Jane asked. "Neal's going to come
here this weekend?"

"Well, just for the day, of course," she
laughed. "He has his plans all made. He will
take the early train and come back that same

evening. I hope you'll have some time to spend with him. That *is* all right, isn't it, dear?"

Whatever Jane stammered satisfied Neal's mother. In a moment it was all over and the phone was back on its hook. Jane stood in a kind of shock. "Help!" she wanted to yell. "Help, help, help!"

Instead, she got control of her trembling and ran downstairs to call Charlotte. After what seemed a ridiculously long time, a voice told her Charlotte was out for the evening. Did Jane want to leave a message?

"No, thank you very much," Jane told the voice, replacing the phone. She couldn't go back into her room and face those flowers. Anyway, she needed someone to talk to . . . anyone!

But who was there? Even if Andy had been there, she was impossible, the way she was acting. She could try to find Toby in the library but that wouldn't help, since Dee was probably with her by now. Jane flushed at the memory of how Dee had looked at her. Dee despised her and Jane wasn't sure she blamed her for it.

She had started upstairs toward Alison's room before she even realized where she was going. She was clear to the top floor, only a few steps from Alison's door, when she heard voices from inside the room. Laughter, a man's laughter, and some other woman's voice, not Alison's.

What did she have to say that was worth interrupting Alison when she was entertaining friends?

What could she say to anyone that would make the heavy hurt place in her chest go away?

CHAPTER TEN

Jane had begun to feel chilled when she talked to Neal's mother on the phone. By the time she got back from the top floor, she was thoroughly cold. Even after putting on all the clothes she could think of, she still felt shivery. Since she couldn't get into her writing assignment, she took out her homework in her other classes. It was hard to concentrate on geometry and biology with Mrs. Worthington's voice echoing in her head.

When she finally heard Toby's laughter on the stairs, she groaned to herself. If Toby was coming back with Dee, that might be worse than having no company at all.

Toby stopped in the doorway, looked at Jane, and laughed. "Boy, do you look like something out of *Little Women*!"

Jane looked down at herself and grinned. With her plush robe over a long flannel gown and a wool shawl on top of that, she probably did. "I bet the library wasn't all that warm, either."

Toby shrugged, pushing her tennis bag onto the floor to make room for Dee on her bed. "I was too busy to notice. Dee was helping me figure out where to start on catching up on my back schoolwork."

Jane looked at Dee thoughtfully. The minute the bed was clear, Dee had flopped on the top of the old army blanket. She was smiling up at Toby with her long legs trailing over the sides of the bed.

"I wouldn't know *where* to start on that," Jane admitted.

"I wouldn't have, either," Toby admitted briskly, sitting backward on her desk chair and looping her arms around the back. "First we had to figure out what was the most important, and start there."

The most important. Neal's mother's voice echoed in Jane's head again as it had all evening. "Don't let him interfere with any of your plans," she had said.

Toby was looking over at her, frowning. "You sure look vacant all of a sudden."

Jane tightened her shoulders. "I was thinking about what you said. I *know* what's the most important thing to me. I just don't know what to do about it." Then, without planning to, she blurted out the chilling news. "Neal is coming to visit this weekend."

"He's what?" Toby asked. "But you have a

date with Cary for the Oakley Prep dance, don't you?"

"I did," Jane said. "I'm not sure I do now."

Dee whistled softly. "I don't know how you can decide which is the most important . . . stop Neal from coming, make peace with Cary, or go back to square one and start all over."

"Couldn't you just tell Neal not to come?" Toby asked.

"It's hard to un-invite somebody you didn't invite," Jane told her.

Dee wasn't angry and scathing as she had been earlier. She made a joke of it. "Sky-writing," she suggested. "Rent an airplane and have the pilot write STAY HOME, NEAL over Neal's campus. If he didn't get your hint, one of the other guys would wise him up."

Jane shook her head. "Neal is hardly a whiz at getting hints. I wrote him that really careful letter, and what did he do? He must have talked to everyone in sight. *My* mom called, and then tonight *his* mom called. They put it in such a way I can't do anything. His mom insisted I not change any plans because he's coming."

"Then don't," Dee said. "Just go to the dance the way you planned."

Jane stared at her. "What if I had the flu or something?"

"There you go!" Dee said. "That's like taking aspirin instead of getting a bad tooth fixed. Postponing is *not* the same as problem-solving."

Jane glared at her. "All right, what would you do, Miss Know-it-all?"

"Spell it out in block letters if necessary. Call him. Send him a telegram. Tell him you just don't have time for him."

"It's only one weekend," Jane protested. "It only happens to be the worst possible weekend."

Dee gave a disgusted snort and rolled herself up off the bed. "I can't believe you, Barrett. Does that mean you're going to keep dragging this out with those two guys indefinitely?" She hooked her book bag over her arm and nodded at Toby. "See you around, Houston."

When she got to the doorway she stopped and looked back at Jane. "What you really deserve is to have both those guys dump *you* at the same time."

"Hey," Maggie protested, as Dee charged into her and Andy outside the door.

"Sorry," Dee said.

Maggie stared after her roommate curiously. "Did we walk in on something?" she asked Andy. Andy, her face still having that distant expression, only shrugged and started taking off her jacket.

"Dee can't stand me," Jane told her. "That's what you walked in on. Dee can't stand me and I don't really blame her for feeling that way. I'm not crazy about myself right now, either."

Toby shook her head. "It's not that she

can't stand you, it's more that she can't *under-*
stand you. The two of you are so different that
you're like the flip side of each other." Then,
realizing that Maggie didn't know what was
going on, she explained. "Boston boyfriend
has invited himself up for the weekend."

"Wow," Maggie said, her eyes wide. "What
a day Saturday is going to be. Faith Thompson
is coming if she can. Neal is coming whether
Jane wants him or not." She paused. "What
about Cary?"

"We're working on that," Toby said. "Or
we will, as soon as we get a good idea. So far
we've only considered ways to keep Neal back
in Boston . . . skywriting, some dread disease
with a Monday cure. He could be roped and
tied at the train station, until it's time for his
return train. . . ."

Andy, having hung up her jacket and put
her hat and scarf away, pulled a bottle of
shampoo from the drawer.

"I have a good idea no one has mentioned,"
she said in a mild tone. "You might try total
honesty with everyone. Not only would it be
something different, but it might even work."
As she spoke, she walked out the door into the
hall.

Maggie let her breath out slowly. "I think
it's time for me to go home," she said quietly.
"Good-night all . . . may peace come to each
of you!"

Toby sat on her bed and looked across at Jane.

"Hey," she said quietly. "Now that everyone on the floor has told you how to mind your own business, what do *you* think you should do?"

Jane sighed. "This is going to sound so weak and worthless after all that passion from Dee and Andy. . . ."

"Never mind them," Toby told her. "You have to do things your own way. So what's the proper Boston girl going to do?"

Jane grinned and nudged her with her slipper. "You're the only person I know who always uses proper before the word Boston. I'm going to have to take you home and straighten you out about my city."

"That's for later. Right now you have to think about Saturday."

"All right," Jane said quietly. "I think I should let Neal come if he wants. . . ." She paused and looked at Toby. "Nobody ever listens when I say he is my *friend* as well as an old boyfriend. Those are different things. Toby, you're always telling me you never had a boyfriend. That's hard to believe. You must have known *some* boys. Didn't you tell me you rode on a bus back and forth to school every day? Were those all girls?"

"Of course not," Toby said. "Other ranchers had sons as well as daughters."

"And there wasn't anybody special?" Jane asked.

Toby shook her head. Then she paused. "Not to me." She laughed at Jane. "I have a

feeling Dad would have liked me to get interested in the Davis kid, Walt, who lives on the
ranch next to ours. I've seen Dad looking at
those fences and thinking what a great *big*
ranch next to ours. I've seen Dad looking at
joined up. But he knows that's a wild dream."

"Why so wild?"

Toby laughed. "For one thing, Walt Davis
can't stand me and I return the favor. I can
outride him and outrope him. I might even
be able to outcuss him if I tried. He comes to
about my shoulder with high-heeled boots on.
His hair is the color of old barn hay, and —"

"Enough, I get the picture." Jane laughed.
"Well, Neal's not short and he's not bad-
looking, and we've always been good friends.
We've had a lot of really good times together.
What I'd like is for him to come visit and
realize that we *still* are friends even though I
have another *boyfriend*. I don't want to hurt
him or get our parents all involved again."

"How do you figure to manage that?" Toby
asked curiously.

Jane nodded, thinking as she talked. "I
would meet his train, and. . . ." She paused.
"I could plan a really full day so I wouldn't
have any time alone with him. That would
tell him more than anything I could say. In
the meantime, I could go and make Cary
listen to how this all started. I could even ask
him if it was all right for me to bring Neal
to the Oakley Prep Dance Saturday night.

I'd have to think of some other ways to keep him busy."

Andy, her hair wrapped in a fluffy towel, had returned to the door. She stood silently a moment. "If you're going to be fair with those guys, I'll do anything I can to help."

Jane looked up, surprised. "Oh, thank you, Andy."

Toby chuckled. "If you think he can understand Texas English, I'll do what *I* can."

"But we'll only pitch in if you're on the level. That means you have to have that talk with Cary first," Andy added.

"Well, there it is," Toby said, with a note of triumph. "We started out looking for the most important thing, and we finally have it. You talk to Cary."

Jane's eyes widened. "But what if Cary won't talk to *me*?"

"*Make* him listen!" Andy said. "He doesn't have any right to jump to conclusions about you. He's got to play fair, too."

When Jane groaned, Toby leaned over and patted her shoulder. "Hey! You're getting the same lesson I got in the library tonight. The most important things are also the hardest."

CHAPTER ELEVEN

Only after that night in the library with Dee did Toby realize how hard it would be to bring her grades back up in time. She couldn't afford to make any mistakes. The next morning she was waiting at the door to the geometry class when the teacher came in.

"Early bird," Mrs. Offutt said, smiling.

Toby nodded, handing her the paper. "I know I'm behind, and I'm sorry," Toby told her. "What's the best way to catch up in a hurry?"

Mrs. Offutt looked at her and laughed. "I was about to say it couldn't be done in my class, October, but I don't believe I dare say that to you."

"No, ma'am," Toby said. "I mean to do it."

Mrs. Offutt motioned her in. "Bring your book. I'll mark the most important concepts. Once you grasp them, you should be able to catch up."

When Toby passed Dee in the hall, she

made a victory sign with her fingers, before darting into the lab early to talk to her biology teacher. Biology and geometry were her really hard subjects. English came easy because she loved to read, and history had always been a favorite.

When she slid in between Maggie and Jane at the lunch table, she showed Jane her marked books. Maggie looked over her shoulder and whistled. "You think you can do all that?"

Toby grinned. "I'm giving it a Texas try."

"I'm not even going to ask what *that* is," Maggie decided aloud.

Toby gathered her books for another grueling night in the library. She leaned to stare out the window of 407. "Remember how light it used to be after dinner when school started?" she asked wistfully. "It's dark out there. That means winter is coming and I'm not even half ready."

Behind her Andy was tugging jeans over her dancing tights. "Everybody talks about how filthy the weather is in Chicago. I don't think this place is going to be any picnic."

When Jane said nothing, Toby glanced over at her. "Are you going to put on your *Little Women* clothes and stay in snug and warm tonight?"

Jane hesitated. "I was thinking about taking the bus into town. . . ."

Toby looked around and her eyes met

Andy's. They *had* to be thinking the same thing. Jane was actually going to go to the diner and talk to Cary Slade. Suddenly, the thought of her doing that made Toby think of bearding a lion in his den. "If you're going to town, I might walk with you," Toby said impulsively. "All study and no exercise rots the brain. And you're forgetting you shouldn't be alone."

Jane looked up at her happily for a brief moment, then she shook her head. "It's nice of you to offer, Toby, but your studies really have to come first for a while."

"The town has a library," Andy said, teasingly. "Canby Hall is not the center of the world's culture."

"Hey, Andy's right," Toby said. "That might be fun. Get your tags on, Jane. I'll just walk down and back."

"You're saying I need to talk to Cary by myself," Jane said quietly.

Toby shrugged. "What do I know about boys?"

"But that's what you meant, wasn't it?"

Toby nodded. "Yeah, I guess I did. I just know that if he was an unbroken pony, you'd take him on by yourself with nobody else around."

Andy paused at the door and laughed. "There she goes again. As Texas goes, so goes the world."

Toby smiled. "We may not be the world," Toby said, "but Dad says boys are like horses.

They're both proud and skittish about who sees them back down."

"Proud and skittish," Andy echoed, letting herself out, thinking solemn thoughts.

The wind was in their faces, walking toward the town. Jane, her head looped in a feathery white mohair scarf, didn't talk at all. By the time they reached Greenleaf, she was walled off in silence. Toby was impressed that Jane, so mild and ladylike, was taking on something that would have scared Toby herself to death. She stopped at the street lamp a half block from the diner. "How do we manage this?" she asked.

At Jane's helpless look, she went on. "I figure we ought to meet at the library," Toby told her. "They could be busy at the diner and you wouldn't have much time to talk." At Jane's stricken expression, she groped for her roommate's mittened hand. "But you could also have a lot of time with Cary. If you're not at the library by nine, I could come by for you."

"Toby, I'm scared."

"Hey." Toby gripped her hand hard. "What's the worst that can happen?"

"I'm too scared to even think about that," Jane mumbled through her scarf.

The diner was half filled when Jane walked in. Cary was at the back, bringing orders of hamburgers and french fries to a rear booth.

He saw her and looked away without acknowledging that he even recognized her. When he had set the orders on the table, he turned and went back to the kitchen without looking her way again. The other boy behind the counter glanced curiously at Cary's back, then approached Jane with a menu and a glass of water. "Booth or counter?" he asked, obviously confused to be waiting on Cary's girlfriend.

"Booth, I guess," she said. "But I just want something hot to drink."

"No problem," he said. "Coffee?"

"Tea," she said, managing to smile. She tightened her arms against her sides to help force the next few words out. "Would you tell Cary I'd like a word with him when he has a minute?"

"Sure," he said, taking the menu back, but not meeting her eyes.

The boy was nervous. When he brought the tea, some had spilled into the saucer, making a dark mush of the vanilla wafer that always came on the side. "Hey, I'm sorry," he said.

She shook her head. "It's okay, it really is."

Almost at once she realized she had chosen the wrong seat in the booth. From where she sat, facing the front of the diner, she could hear the swinging door to the kitchen open and shut, but she couldn't see who was coming in and out. But she knew that Cary had to be making some of those trips.

The tea was terribly hot at first so she sipped

it slowly. The minutes continued to pass and
Cary didn't come. The two couples in the
back booth finished their meal and came to
the front of the diner, putting their coats and
scarves on. The other boy took their money
at the register, even though Cary had waited
on them. Seeing her eyes on him, he looked
over at Jane. "More tea?"

Jane nodded. "Did you give Cary my
message?"

He flushed a deep ruddy color. "I guess he's
been real busy," he mumbled. When he came
back with the fresh cup of tea, he grinned
shyly at her. "See, I didn't spill any this time."

"You're great," Jane said, her heart sinking.
Now she would have to wait for this cup of
tea to cool. Then she would drink it. Then
what? And all this time Cary was lurking back
there in the kitchen, avoiding her. Jane set
down her cup and got up. She was almost at
the kitchen door when Cary came through.
Seeing her, he stopped suddenly, his face set in
that hard, cold expression he'd had the night
Gigi had been in the diner.

"Hello, Cary," Jane said, forcing her voice
to stay level. "I wanted to talk to you."

"I'm on duty," he said coldly.

"I realize that," she said. "This will only
take a minute."

"I don't have a minute," he said, stepping
to the side to walk around her.

"Cary," she said. "You're not being fair."

He laughed loudly enough that a customer

at one of the stools looked around. "*You* are going to give *me* lessons in fairness?" he asked.

She felt her own face blaze with color. Toby's comment about pride and the pony came back. Maybe she was like an unbroken colt herself, but his making such a public scene infuriated her. She looked at him soberly, then nodded. "Maybe you're right," she told him. "Perhaps *manners* is something *you* should take lessons in."

She walked past him, laid the money for the tea on the table, and added an extra dollar bill to it. When she looked around, Cary was still staring after her. "The tip," she said coldly, "is for the other person."

The cold night air felt wonderful on her hot cheeks, as she plunged out the door and started for the library.

Toby was just gathering up her things when Jane walked in. "That bad?" Toby asked after a glance at Jane's face.

Jane nodded. "He wouldn't even talk to me."

Toby scraped to her feet angrily. "That was my mistake. I should have gone with you. I was thinking about horses and you were dealing with a stubborn old mule."

Twice during the night Toby was wakened by Jane's restlessness. Jane tossed and turned in her bed. Once, when she heard Jane crying softly, Toby rose on one elbow, and whispered her name, only to realize that Jane was sobbing in her sleep. Toby lay angrily silent. Cary wasn't worth all that. Cary wasn't worth *any* of that. And it was already Wednesday, which meant there were only two more days before Saturday, when Neal would come and the Oakley Prep Dance would take place.

The roommates dressed in silence the next morning. Jane was the last to be ready to go down to breakfast and Andy looked at her curiously as she followed them out the door. In the dining room, they took their trays to the table and sat down before anyone said anything. Then Toby looked over at Jane. "Feeling better this morning?" she asked quietly.

"I'm fine," Jane said.

"Then talking to Cary didn't work?" Andy asked.

Instant tears came to Jane's eyes. "No," she said softly. "It didn't work. But that's okay. I tried."

"And now you feel *fine*?" Andy asked.

Jane nodded, looking puzzled at her question.

Andy shrugged and glanced fleetingly at Toby. "We're different in Chicago. When we put on shoes that don't match, we're anything but fine!"

Jane frowned and looked down at her feet. She groaned and stood up to dump her uneaten breakfast tray. Andrea was right. She had a brown loafer on her left foot and a gray one on the right.

"Wait," Toby cried. "Eat something. Take your toast. I'll butter you a muffin!"

Jane shook her head. "It's too late. I have to rush."

"Jane," Toby yelled after her.

Andrea put her hand on Toby's arm. "Let her go, Toby, I think she doesn't want to talk."

CHAPTER TWELVE

Even following Mrs. Offutt's suggestions, Toby couldn't figure out one of the back lessons. She raced over to the Main Building to get a minute with the teacher before class. She was waiting outside the door when Gigi Norton and her friends walked by. Gigi's crimson cashmere sweater exactly matched the silk scarf she had tied around sleek black hair. Her walk screamed "Look at me!"

But she was looking at Toby.

"Look at that!" she laughed. "It's Texas style to wear the same wrinkled shirt three days in a row."

Toby felt herself flush. Gigi was right, she had forgotten to change outfits all week. But getting her grades caught up to stay at Canby Hall was a lot more important than showing off clothes. "My goodness!" Toby drawled. "I thought I was being high style. I *know* those are the same false eyelashes you were batting around yesterday!"

Mrs. Offutt was unlocking the door. Toby got inside without hearing what Gigi was sputtering to her friends.

"You look happy this morning, October," the teacher said, opening the book to Toby's marker.

"I just made my own day," Toby said, grinning back at her.

Even though the rest of the day went well (Toby got a 97 on a pop history test and an A– on her English paper), she couldn't wait to get back to Baker House and change her wilted plaid shirt.

The sun had shone early that Thursday, but by the end of the last class it was windy and cold. Toby raced between her last class and Baker House with her head down, trying to keep the wind from whipping her face. She was almost to the front steps when someone called her name. As she hesitated and looked around, Cary Slade stepped from the trees almost in front of her and caught her arm. "Hey, Texas," he said. "I want to talk to you."

"My name is October and I *don't* want to talk to you," she said, twisting away.

"Come on," he coaxed. "I've been waiting here a half hour and I'm freezing. I can't find Jane."

She looked at him levelly. "She was in the diner last night," she reminded him.

He ducked his head and sighed. "So I made a fool of myself last night."

"You were an old mule last night," she told him.

He grinned. "Trust a Texan to call it like it is. I was sorry the minute she left but it was too late. I couldn't leave the job. But I really do need to talk to her. I've been waiting here all this time and she hasn't come back from classes."

Toby looked at him thoughtfully. He looked good and chilled to the bone. But it was funny he had missed Jane. She usually got back to Baker only a few minutes before Toby herself arrived. "I'll check for you," she agreed grudgingly. "Come on inside."

Mrs. Betts was passing out mail to a bunch of girls. A flower delivery, draped in green, stood at her side. When Mrs. Betts was free, she looked up at Toby. "No mail, I'm afraid," she said. "Unless you want to...." She reached for the flowers. Then, glancing at Cary, she drew her hand back.

"I'll take Jane's flowers up when I go," Toby told her. So let Cary get the whole picture, let him know what kind of competition he had! "Has Jane come in from class yet?"

Mrs. Betts shook her head. "She came in a little after noon. She wasn't feeling well and was released from classes."

"Anything special?" Toby asked, glaring at Cary.

Mrs. Betts frowned. "Probably a touch of flu. She looked really washed out." She glanced at Cary. "I could ring the hall phone on her floor. If she's awake, she'll hear it."

Toby waited silently until Mrs. Betts had Jane on the line, then took the phone herself. "Cary Slade is down here," she said. "But you don't have to talk to him unless you want to."

"Hey," Cary protested behind her, reaching for the phone. Toby shoved his hand away. "Okay, Jane. I'll tell him."

"She's a sucker for punishment," Toby said, turning to Cary. "She'll come down to the lounge right away."

"Listen, Toby," he said, "come in with me a minute. I need to talk to you." She hesitated before following him. Since some of the girls who had returned earlier from classes had the tv blaring at the end of the room, Toby and Cary stood in a quiet corner near the door.

"Okay. Talk," Toby said, standing very straight and glaring at him.

"Boy, you don't see but one side of anything, do you?" he asked, suddenly showing his annoyance at her. "How do you think a guy feels when he finds out a girl is getting the rush from some guy out of town? How do I know she's not stringing me along? What kind of a guy would I be if I didn't get jealous? What do you expect a guy to do when he doesn't know where he stands with a girl?"

Jane spoke quietly from the doorway. "He could let her explain."

Cary turned with such a look of relief on his face that Toby backed off, lifted a hand that neither of them noticed, and whispered, "Peace!" to herself as she faded out of the room into the hall.

"About last night," Cary began. "I *was* mean." As he spoke, a group of girls came through the door, slowing down to stare at him and Jane as they passed. "Listen," he interrupted himself. "My car's outside. It's a little cold but you could have my jacket."

This is wrong, Jane told herself. I'm being awfully weak after the way he was last night, but he *has* apologized. . . . As she hesitated, Gigi Norton came into the hall and started up the stairs with her friends. When she saw Jane and Cary, Gigi motioned them toward the lounge.

"Your car then," she agreed, letting him slip his letter jacket over her shoulders as they started for the front door.

Out in the car, Cary turned to her and took both her hands. "See Jane, what you have to understand is how much the whole thing took me off guard. Just when I was sure you and I had *really* gotten it together, I hear all this stuff. Flowers every ten minutes? Come on. Who can compete with that? I knew you must have had a guy back home, or a lot of them, for all I knew. Maybe you even liked them better than me."

He was going on and on and getting nowhere. Jane pulled one hand free and held it up. "Give me a minute," she told him. "First off, you need to know there were never a lot of guys. There was only Neal."

He groaned. "When you say it that way, I suddenly wish there *had* been a lot of guys."

"Come on, Cary," she pleaded. "It's only fair to let me explain." He listened thoughtfully as she told him about her folks, and Neal's folks, and how it had always been between the families. "That letter was the hardest thing I ever wrote in my life. Then *my* mother called, and *his* mother called."

Cary groaned and struck his forehead with the palm of one hand. "I would really be angry at my mom for a trick like that. She wouldn't dare."

"Mrs. Worthington dared," Jane said. Then, catching her breath for courage, she plunged on. "She also dared to tell me that Neal is coming here this weekend to see me."

"This weekend?" His voice rose dangerously. "The weekend of our dance? Doesn't he know how to take NO for an answer?"

She shook her head. "And neither do either of our folks."

He turned back in his seat and gripped the steering wheel with both hands. "Jane," he said finally. "I don't really know how much you like this guy down deep inside. You're letting him come."

"Neal and I have been friends all our lives," she told him again.

Cary turned his wrist to look at his watch,

then groaned. "I have to go. I'll barely make it to the diner on time." He turned and looked at her. "So what are you going to do?"

"I don't *know* what to do," she wailed.

"All this time you keep repeating over and over that this guy is your *friend*. That's a good enough place to start. If this guy is your friend like you say, treat him like one. Get him a date and they can double with us on Saturday night!"

Jane stared at Cary, open-mouthed.

"See?" he said. "You don't like the thought of him with another girl. Do you wonder I'm confused?" Then, hastily, "I really have to go. You don't mind walking back into the hall alone, do you?"

She opened the door and got out, shaking her head.

"Keep the jacket till I see you," he called. "But let me know what to expect. I'm not into your surprises."

Jane stood huddled in his jacket, watching him throw his car into gear. "And don't forget Neal's flowers waiting at the desk for you," he called back to her.

She watched him drive away, wanting to yell at him and cry at the same time.

Toby and Andy both looked around when Jane walked in, wearing Cary's jacket and carrying Neal's flowers. Jane set the flowers down with a thump and shrugged the jacket off onto the floor.

"For anyone else, dropping that jacket might have significance," Andy observed. "For Jane, it means she got warm. The audience needs clearer signals to understand how 407's private soap opera is progressing."

"Be nice," Toby said sharply. "She's been sick today."

"I'd be sick, too, if I flopped and groaned all night like she did," Andy replied, but with sympathy in her voice.

"Quit talking about me as if I were not here," Jane ordered so firmly that both Andy and Toby stared at her. "I don't need an audience rating," she added a little more quietly. "I need help."

"We tried to help," Toby protested.

Jane nodded. "Right! You suggested I write a 'Dear Neal' letter and I did. You suggested I explain everything to Cary, and I've done that. Cary made a suggestion and I need help to carry it out."

"So?" Andy asked, interested in spite of herself.

"He says I should get a date for Neal for Saturday night's dance."

"Hey," Toby said. "Good thinking."

"Does that mean you volunteer?" Jane asked swiftly.

Toby's jaw fell. "Me? You've got to be kidding." Then, seeing that Jane wasn't, she began to pile excuses one on top of the other. "You know how much back schoolwork I have to catch up on. Why, even if I study all night every night. . . ."

"Okay," Jane said quietly, looking at Andy. "You?"

"To quote our Texas friend with a slight correction in grammar, 'You have to be kidding,'" Andy said. "He might not want to go to a dance with . . . me."

"Thank you both for your support," Jane said. She turned, picked up Cary's jacket, and walked out the door.

Jane didn't appear at dinner. When Dee stopped by on the way to the library, she found Toby very depressed. "What's your problem?" Dee asked. "Surely it's not grades again?"

Toby shook her head. "The grades are staggering to their feet. But I hate it when I can't do stuff to help my friends."

"Who did you let down today?" Dee asked briskly.

"Jane. She needs a date for her Boston boyfriend on Saturday night," Toby told her.

"That's not all that girl needs," Dee told her. "She caught Maggie late this afternoon. She's made up a schedule to keep that guy from Boston busy all day Saturday." Dee laughed. "Poor Maggie. Jane asked her to play doubles in tennis that morning. Maggie doesn't know one end of a racket from the other."

Toby suppressed an instant of temptation.
What fun it would be to play tennis. But she
probably wasn't good enough, and she did
have plenty of studying still to do. "Isn't that
the day Maggie is hoping Faith Thompson
will come visit?" Toby asked.

Dee nodded. "She's still hoping, but she
hasn't heard anything definite yet. In the
meantime, Maggie is supposed to paint scenery for the play that morning."

"This is going to be one wild Saturday,"
Toby said. "In fact, it would probably be a
good weekend to be out of town . . . say, back
home in Texas!"

When Toby got home from the library,
Andrea was visiting next door and there was
no sign of Jane. Toby set down her books and
drifted down the hall looking for her.

She had given up and was on her way back
to 407 when she heard slow steps on the stairs
coming down. Jane, looking very dejected,
was dragging Cary's jacket behind her.

"Missed you," Toby told her, waiting at
the bottom of the stairs. "I looked all over."

"I went up to see Alison," Jane told her.
"I thought she might come up with some
bright ideas to fill my schedule for Neal
Saturday."

"Did she?"

"She helped a little. She suggested I take
a bunch, him included, to Pizza Pete's for
lunch. As slow as service is in there on Satur-

day, that would burn two hours at least."
Jane shrugged. "But she didn't have any ideas
on a date for him. She did suggest I ask Dee
to fill in at tennis, but I can't do that."

"Why not?" Toby asked.

Jane looked at her. "You can't ask somebody who hates you to do you a favor."

"Is Neal some big prize-winning player?"
Toby asked.

Jane looked at her, startled, then shook her
head. "He plays okay, but he's really into
sailing. Why?"

Toby felt herself flush. "If there aren't any
stars in the game, maybe *I* could fill in." The
minute the words were out she wanted them
back. She wasn't good enough. How could she
offer to give up study time for tennis, after
she had used that as an excuse to keep from
going to the dance with Neal?

"Oh, Toby," Jane cried, seizing her by the
arms. "Would you? How wonderful!"

"But I couldn't do the dance," Toby put in
swiftly.

"I know," Jane said. "You are *such* a great
friend."

Toby turned away so Jane wouldn't see her
blush. Inside, she worried about all the
trouble being a great friend was getting her
into.

CHAPTER THIRTEEN

That Saturday morning Maggie rapped on the door of Room 407 before anyone was up. Jane, who was awake but dreading the day so much that she couldn't make her body move, called to ask who it was.

"Maggie," the answer came. "Can I come in?"

"Only if it's a matter of life or death," Toby growled from under her army blanket.

"It is," Maggie assured her, opening the door at once. "I'll just simply die if I don't get to see Faith today."

Andy rose on her elbows to glare at Maggie's eager face. "Canby Hall has been here forever with girls sharing this room. I refuse to go sleepless because some 'old girl' is coming back." She snuggled down in her blue flannel nightgown.

"Faith Thompson isn't just any old girl," Maggie protested. "Faith is simply the most wonderful, beautiful, wise, talented person you'll ever know, after my sister Dana, of course. And it *is* morning."

"Spare us the adjectives," Andy groaned. "Just speak your piece so we can go back to sleep."

"I have to work on the backdrop today. I'll come home the first minute I can. Will everyone tell Faith I'm coming and not to leave until I see her?"

"Everyone will tell her that," Toby muttered.

"Two or three times," Andy said. "Now go!"

The room was silent for a moment after Maggie shut the door. Then Andy spoke again in a murderous tone. "I hear movement," she warned. "I hear quiet, sneaky, human movement in my sleeping space. Will the intruder identify itself before I attack it?"

"It's me," Jane admitted in a whisper. "I have a train to meet."

Andy groaned and pulled her pillow over her head. Toby, watching, seized the moment to creep out of her bed and make her getaway.

Once they were safely inside the washroom, standing at the sinks, Toby and Jane broke into laughter. "I forgot how hilarious Andy can be," Toby admitted. "Lately, though, she's only funny when she's half unconscious. Maybe we could keep her asleep all the time, just for the fun of having the old Andy back."

Jane shook her head. "I've almost given up hope." Then she looked at Toby curiously. "Why are *you* up so early? You don't have a train to meet."

Toby grinned. "I tossed all night worrying about disgracing you in this tennis game today. I haven't hit a single ball in a whole week. The only thing I could think of to do was to slip out and warm up early."

"This is just a friendly game," Jane protested. "Not Wimbledon."

"I say it's Wimbledon," Toby declared flatly.

Jane shook her head and grinned as she bent down to brush her teeth.

Jane was at the station early. As she watched the big second hand of the clock move toward the time of Neal's arrival, she tightened her hands in her lap. She was scared. She had drifted out of sleep with an excited feeling that she hadn't been able to identify for a moment. When she did, she was wide awake and shocked at herself.

She had been excited and happy because Neal was coming. But she liked Cary. How could she like Cary and feel this excitement at the thought of seeing Neal? Was Cary right? Was she unsure of how she felt about Neal?

"It's because we have always been such good friends," she told herself, as the whistle of the arriving train drowned out the ticking of the station clock.

Neal was the first passenger to swing off the train. He started looking around while he was still on the steps. Jane couldn't even wave. It was just so good to see his lean angular face with his dark eyes searching for her with such anticipation. His smile, the moment he saw her, filled her with simultaneous happiness and shame. Then he was there, grabbing her close. He didn't say anything for a moment, just held her tight.

When she got herself loose, she looked up at him, suddenly self-conscious. "Have you had breakfast?" she asked.

He laughed. "You talk like a parent. The question is 'Do you want to eat?,' and you know I always do." He glanced around. "How about the little diner?"

At her stricken look, he put his arm around her shoulder. "Oops. You told me your new friend had a job in town. Is that where he works?"

At her nod, he shrugged. "No problem. They almost always make great breakfasts in little inns like you have here. How about we try that?"

He looked around the town eagerly as they walked toward the inn. At the front door he reached around Jane and opened it for her, smiling down into her eyes. "Relax, Janie. This is *not* the end of the world. The end of

the world would come if we blew this many
years of friendship. Right?"

"Right," she breathed, beginning to feel
some hope for this day for the first time. How
had she managed to forget what a really nice
guy Neal was?

Toby practiced hard an hour before going
back to the room. Only then did she realize
the first thing she had failed to do. Her wail
brought Andy up out of her homework with
a start.

"I don't know how to dress," she said. "I
should have asked Jane what to put on."

Andy looked at her. "For what?"

"For tennis, of course," Toby said. "I've
never played with real people before."

Andy grunted. "What do you wear when
you play with unreal people?"

"You know what I mean," Toby rebuked
her. "I've only played with coaches. And when
you see tennis played on tv, the women have
on shorts and polo shirts, or bouncy little
white skirts with low cut — "

"And those games are played in October
in New England?" Andy asked.

"Well. . . ." Toby hesitated.

"Put on your blue and gold Canby Hall
warm-up suit and forget it," Andy said. "Anyone out there with bare knees today is going
to have chilblain."

"I don't even know what that is," Toby
said glumly.

"Wear your shorts out there and you'll find out," Andy said, disappearing back into her book.

Toby was ready for the tennis game thirty minutes early. She walked around the campus and down to a nearby farm to look at the animals. The last time she had gone there, the orchard trees had been filled with fruit. Now they were covered with bright leaves, except for a shriveled apple here and there that a pair of crows were fighting over. The barn smelled like her barn at home. She turned to walk swiftly toward the tennis courts to ward off the wave of homesickness that threatened to overwhelm her.

Andy had been right about the cold. Toby's warm-up suit felt snug in the chill wind blowing off the skating pond. She sat on the bench and watched a pair of ducks turn upside down to search the bottom of the pond for food. She didn't notice Jane had come to the court until she called out. Jane stood between two boys, both wearing warm-up suits as Jane was. The first of her two questions was answered.

The answer to the second question stopped her in her tracks as the tall man to the right of Jane turned and waved for her to hurry.

Randy Crowell.

"No," she groaned aloud to herself. Jane *couldn't* have asked Randy Crowell to fill out the foursome. But Jane didn't know how bad her crush on Randy was. Toby's feet were un-

steady on the cold ground as she crossed to
them.

There were introductions, with Neal's manners reminding Toby of a British movie.
Maybe that was the answer. If she could convince herself she was playing against an actor,
she wouldn't even notice Randy beside her.

They warmed up a long time with lots of
laughter. Toby was furious that her tenseness
simply wouldn't leave. She knew her move-
ments were exaggerated and half of the balls
she intended for Jane landed on Neal's side
of the court. Maybe she could get control of
herself when the game began, she told herself
desperately.

Another maybe disappeared fast. She and
Randy were down five games before Toby
realized what was happening. Being so far
behind only made her worse.

"Relax, Toby," Randy said warmly as they
changed courts. "Tennis is only a game."

She couldn't summon any more answer than
a groan.

Jane and Neal had won the first set six
games to one, when four girls walked onto
the next court. Gigi Norton and three of her
clones. That was it, Toby knew. If she had
been stiff before, she would freeze solid now.

Neal served the first ball of the second set
and Toby returned it with sheer luck. She
and Randy lost that game and the next, before
Gigi's laughter reached Toby from the other
court. She didn't really hear what Gigi said,

but it was apparently very funny, and clearly spoken in an exaggerated Texas accent. Toby blazed with fury. It wasn't enough that she couldn't relax with Randy, she had to deal with Gigi's ridicule at the same time.

When Randy handed her the balls to serve, she felt the heat of her fury gather behind her stroke. She'd show Gigi.

"Wow," Neal called. "Warn a guy, will you?"

Toby stared over at him.

"That was a winning serve," Randy laughed. "Now get Jane."

Jane did return the serve but barely. Toby had time to get to the net and angle the ball off past Neal's running attempt to catch it.

The games weren't all one way after that, but Toby played with growing confidence. After she and Randy took the second set, they went to six even on the third before Neal won the game.

Randy turned to Toby, shook her hand, and then took both her hands. "You are great! I didn't even know you played the game."

"She didn't until this fall," Jane said with a proud smile. "Isn't she something?"

Neal was staring at her. "You have to be kidding," he said. "You mean you got a tennis game like that in one season?"

Toby could only nod, and hope they wouldn't notice the fierce way she blushed from all their praise.

"She's no slouch on a horse, either," Randy

added. "Come on, Neal and I will walk you two back to your house."

Toby didn't look back at the courts. Gigi Norton didn't really matter. Strangely, not even Randy mattered that much. In fact, she realized it was only after she had forgotten about Randy that she had really played. She knew now she could play the game. Back home she would have let out a war whoop, but a glance at Neal stopped that in her throat as she fell into step beside him.

Toby was glad that Neal was an easy talker. Except for Randy, and then only when the subject was horses, she had trouble talking with boys. Neal was different. "I'm interested in how you developed such a good game so fast," he said. "Tell me."

She looked at him suspiciously. "You have a good game, too."

"Thank you, but that's different," he said. "My game has been drilled into me all my life, like Jane's has. We both play tennis because it's something you learn to do. But your game is different, as if you really care."

"I do," Toby said. "I like to beat hard things."

His eyes were a remarkable color as he studied her. And even in a warm-up suit and tennis shoes, he managed to look properly Ivy League. And his talk! If her dad could see this guy with his proper manners and strange stiffness, with his funny tight accent and formal phrases, he would laugh himself silly and use words like "dude" and "dandified."

Her dad would be wrong.

"You like to beat hard things?" Neal repeated. When he smiled, he was more than nice-looking, he was really handsome. "I know what you mean by that, Toby, because I feel the same way about sailing."

She never did tell him how she developed her game. She wouldn't have had a chance if she wanted to. He told her about his boat and how hard it had been to realize that his life was in his own hands when he sailed. "It's hard," he said, "but really exciting."

Randy startled her by interrupting. "Thanks again for the game, Toby. It was great." She was astonished to see they had already reached Baker House. Randy turned to Neal. "Come on, Neal, I'll give you a lift back to my place to change."

Jane talked happily all the way upstairs. She had been so proud of Toby's game. She couldn't tell Toby how much she appreciated her taking time away from her studies for those three full sets. She was so pleased that Neal had enjoyed her so much. "It's really nice when your friends like each other," she went on.

Toby just nodded, still amazed at what she had discovered. Who would think that a guy who came off as such a stuffed shirt could be just as nice and fair and human as the next guy? She had something to explain to her dad some time. Maybe you could judge a Hereford by the way it looked, but the same didn't hold for people.

CHAPTER FOURTEEN

Earlier, Andy had been relieved to have Saturday off to catch up on her homework. The stage was in use for the production of the back drops, so no dance practice was scheduled at all. She was glad she wouldn't be yelled at once all day with that constant, "Smile, Cord, smile!"

The phone rang, interrupting her thoughts. It was Maggie from the auditorium.

"It's time for Faith's train to be in," Maggie said. "Is she there?"

"No sign of her," Andy said.

Maggie wailed, "You *will* give her my message?"

Andy assured Maggie she would. But in what seemed like no time at all, Maggie called again, She asked hopefully, "Has she called?"

"No word," Andy said, making no effort to keep her annoyance out of her voice. "Can I call you there?"

Maggie groaned. "The only phone is out

here in the front office and nobody's here to answer."

Andy shrugged. So Dana's old roommate wasn't going to make it after all. What was the big deal?

The dorm was quiet except for a stereo thrumming rhythm without sound through the ceiling of the room below. The furnace breathed in and out as Andy worked. Since she hadn't heard any footsteps in the hall, the rap on the open door startled her.

She looked up and blinked. The best-looking young black woman she had seen since leaving Chicago was standing in the doorway. This girl was tall and so classically dressed that she gave an instant impression of high style. She hitched the leather strapped camera that hung from her shoulder, and smiled with such charm and presence that Andy leaped to her feet without thinking.

"Hi there," the stranger said. "I'm Faith Thompson. I wonder if you know where I could find Maggie Morrison."

"Faith," Andy repeated, staring at her. What had Maggie said about this girl? "The most wonderful, beautiful, wise, talented person?" She looked all of that. Andy caught her breath and smiled back.

"Of course," she said. "Come in. Maggie has been a basket case for fear she wouldn't get to see you. I'm Andrea Cord from Chicago."

Faith stepped forward and took her hand

in a cool, firm grip. "It's great to meet you. It's great to be back." She looked around the room, examining everything carefully. "Blue walls? I'm not just being nosy. I promised Dana and Shelley I would write and tell them exactly how our room looked. The answer is different . . . but great," she added quickly.

Andy nodded. "She and the rest of the crew are working on the stage drop for the musical," she explained. "Maybe we could catch her at the auditorium."

Faith turned her wrist to study her watch. "That's probably the best; I don't have a lot of time." She grinned. "I wouldn't have even gotten here at all if it hadn't been for Mr. Kreevitch."

Andy frowned. The name rang a bell, but a distant one.

"The Canby Hall grounds keeper, Bernard Kreevitch," Faith explained. "What a neat couple he and his wife are. I couldn't have shot the landscape picture that got me into this show in Boston without his help. When I wrote him about it and told him I would be there, he and Mrs. Kreevitch insisted on meeting my train and bringing me out here this morning. They'll drive me back to Boston because they want to see the show."

Andy reached for her jacket. "I'll walk over to the auditorium with you. I'm sure you know the way." She laughed. "But I'd like to."

Mrs. Betts delayed them in the lobby. "Faith," she cried, coming around the desk to fold Faith in a vast hug. "How wonderful it is to see you. You look. . . ."

"Older?" Faith asked, hopefully. "College can do that to you."

"More beautiful than ever," Mrs. Betts corrected her. "Give your family my best, hear?"

Faith's steps slowed as they walked toward the auditorium. "This place is so full of memories for me!" she said softly. Then, turning, she smiled at Andy. "How are things going for you?"

"As well as can be expected," Andy said, shrugging. "I like it fine, except for that same old problem."

"Problem?" Faith asked, looking at her in a puzzled way.

"Just ordinary garden variety discrimination," Andy said. "I should get used to prejudice against black girls. I guess I'm a slow learner."

"At Canby Hall?" Faith's voice rose. "Give me an example."

"I only have one example but it's enough," Andy said.

By the time Andy finished telling about the auditions and losing the leading role to another girl just because she was white, they were approaching the steps of the auditorium.

Faith stopped dead in her tracks. "You *have* to be wrong, Andy," she said positively. "Your color can't be the reason you lost that role.

Canby Hall doesn't operate that way. I felt like you, when I first came here, but I learned it wasn't so. Everyone isn't going to be your best friend, but there's no discrimination as far as marks and honors and leading roles go."

"That's easy enough for you to say," Andy said, angered that Faith would take sides against her. "You're out of here and in college where there are a lot of black kids."

Faith frowned. "What you're doing is really dangerous, Andrea. It scares me. If another girl got the starring role in a show here, it was because she outdanced you. The way to win at Canby Hall is simply to be the best."

Andy stood very still, trying to control her blazing anger. "All right. You know so much! Explain why I get yelled at two to one over every other dancer in rehearsal?" She mimicked the director's tone, "Smile, Cord, smile."

Faith touched her arm. "Listen, Andrea. If you're walking in there feeling discriminated again, what kind of a smile can you have on your face? Forget your hurt feelings. Be honest about your own limitations. You can always get better and better."

The door of the auditorium burst open as Maggie, trailing her coat behind her, charged down the stairs shouting, "Faith! You came. You came!"

Faith smiled up at Maggie but she caught Andy by the shoulders in a quick hug. "Think about it, Andy. If you're the best, you'll get top billing. And there's always another year. . . ."

Andy walked along silently as Maggie chattered steadily to Faith. As they approached Baker House, they heard the blare of a truck horn. Mr. Kreevitch and his wife were waiting to drive Faith back to Boston.

Maggie waved wildly as the truck pulled away, but Faith's eyes were on Andy, as was her smile.

The noon delivery had brought Andy a package from Chicago. When Jane and Toby got to the room, Andy and Maggie were gorging themselves on cheese popcorn while they talked about Faith's visit.

"So how was the tennis?" Maggie asked, looking up.

"Super," Toby said, fighting the second impulse of the day to let out a Texas war whoop.

"It was wonderful," Jane agreed. "You should have seen Toby here. . . ."

"Wait," Toby cried, stripping off her sweat suit. "I can't stand any more praise. I'm giddy now."

"She really was wonderful," Jane was saying.

"One more thing," Toby said, "before I forget. If you still want somebody to go to the dance with Neal tonight, I'm game."

The room was silent. Andy and Jane stared

at each other in amazement. "Did you hear that?" Jane whispered.

Andy nodded. "I didn't believe it, but I heard it."

"Maybe I missed something," Maggie said, looking from one of them to the other.

"Cornelius Worthington III," Jane said carefully, "is one of the best friends I've ever had. But, Maggie dear, he is also a proper Bostonian."

"To put it bluntly," Andy added. " 'Mr. Boston-stuffed-shirt' and 'I'm only-at-home-on-the-range-Toby' are the most unlikely couple in the history of the world."

Maggie giggled softly. "But it solves Jane's problem, doesn't it?"

CHAPTER FIFTEEN

"Twice in one day?" Andy asked Toby. "Twice in a single day you are going into hysterics over what to wear? I don't believe you."

Toby slumped onto her bed, shaking her head. "I don't believe myself. Andy, how could I have done that? How could I have told Jane I would go out with Cornelius Worthington the Third? I just lost my head. I just liked him. I just thought he was a nice guy. But I don't know how to date."

Andy sighed, closed her book, and left her desk to sit cross-legged on her bed, studying Toby.

"Okay," she said with an air of resignation. "Do you know how to dance?"

"I can square dance," Toby said doubtfully.

"Show me how you do it," Andy ordered. Toby rose obediently and did a few steps, whirling and stepping in and out. Andy watched her curiously, then asked, "Why are you holding your arm up like that?"

"That's for the other couple to pass under."

"Okay," Andy said, wisely. "We'll work on that later. So you can tell Neal that you can't dance, but you really enjoy his company."

"I bet he can dance," Toby said.

"Of course he can dance," Andy said. She started to add that rich boys and girls like Neal and Jane were taught how to do everything before they were old enough to need it. Remembering what Faith had said, she held her tongue. "Since Neal will be able to dance, tell him to go get a partner. I know," she added brightly, "tell him to go dance so you can watch him and learn how."

Toby flushed. "He did tell me I was a fast learner. Not in those words, of course." Then she frowned in doubt. "But what do I *wear*, while I am sending him out there to dance with other people?"

"You must have *one* party dress," Andy said.

"I hate it," Toby said sullenly.

"Never mind what you think of it," Andy said. "Show it to me."

"I *really* hate it," Toby said, pulling a box off the shelf of her closet.

"Neiman-Marcus." Andy read the box label. "It can't be all bad. If you hate it so much, why did you bring it to school?"

"My aunt in Dallas sent it to me. She goes

through my closet when she comes to visit us at the ranch. She thinks a man like Dad doesn't know what a girl needs. She's wrong. He keeps me in Levis. If I'd left this dress at home and she'd found out, she would have thrown a fit." As she spoke, she pulled the dress out and held it up. "Look at this ugly thing. It's the same color as my hair."

"It really is," Andy agreed. "That's one way to go. I wish she had gone for contrast and bought green to match your eyes, but that isn't bad. I have copper earrings about that color you could borrow. How about shoes?"

Toby sighed and pulled a pair of low-heeled brown pumps from the closet.

"That dress *really* has a nice skirt," Andy said thoughtfully, "Full and swirly. What's that thing at the bottom of the V of the blouse?"

"Fake flower," Toby said sullenly.

"That has to go," Andy said. "It's probably just tacked on with a few threads, anyway. Come on, try it on."

"Hey," Andy said when the dress slid down over Toby's slender body. "You look about two inches around in that, just great. All except your hair."

Toby peered at herself. "My hair's always like that."

Andy rose and reached for Toby's brush. "You aren't *always* on a date." After a few painful strokes, she caught Toby's curls back into a glowing mound at the nape of her neck.

"Hey, hand me that flower." She had barely finished pining the silk blossom in Toby's mass of red curls when Jane spun in at the door.

"It's almost time for Neal to come by . . . Toby!" Jane stopped in the doorway with her mouth open. "You look fabulous!"

"Andy did it," Toby said, looking at Jane with suspicion to be sure she wasn't being kidded.

"Andy, you're wonderful!" Jane said. "Turn around, Toby. What a transformation! Neal won't believe his eyes."

"I can't dance," Toby told her.

"Nobody really dances to the music of Cary's group," Jane told her. "You move your feet, and jiggle, and keep time."

Andy stepped back and looked Toby over carefully. "Makeup. You need some makeup."

"No!" Toby shouted. "You're not going to put a lot of gook all over *my* face."

"Not a lot," Andy said. "Just a little bit." She dug in her closet and came out with her kit of stage makeup.

Toby retreated anxiously.

"Let her," Jane said. "She knows how to do it, Toby."

Reluctantly, Toby let Jane sit her down on a chair and Andrea carefully applied light makeup on Toby's tense face. She added very pale, green eyeshadow that brought out the green of Toby's eyes and then a film of lip gloss to Toby's tightly shut mouth.

"Open your mouth a little, Toby," Andy ordered.

"If I open my mouth, I'll scream," Toby said.

"Okay, scream, but open your mouth," Andy said, carefully adding the lip gloss.

When Andrea was finished both she and Jane oohed and ahed over Toby. Toby fearfully went to the mirror and looked in. "That's me?" she asked. "Not bad. Not bad at all."

Jane had felt a little fear about Cary's behavior ever since she agreed to bring Neal to the dance. Once she got there, the feeling disappeared at once. Cary wasn't just good . . . he was fabulous! When she and Toby walked in with Neal, Cary left the bandstand and came over to be introduced. He couldn't have been nicer. He even asked Neal about some friends he had at Neal's prep school.

"My date insists she can't dance," Neal told Cary. "She has come to watch and learn."

Cary looked at Toby and grinned. "Great idea. And there's nothing a musician likes better than a dedicated listener." As he spoke, someone called him from the bandstand. "Oops," he said. "Back to the sweat shop. Talk to you later."

When the music began and the dancers began to move out onto the floor, Neal looked uncertainly at Toby. "Are you sure you want me to leave you?"

"Positive," she said. "I'll have fun watching."

"Well, if you're sure." He hesitated and turned to Jane. "Jane, may I have this dance?"

Of course it had to be a very slow dance, one of the few that Cary's band would play all evening. Naturally Jane and Neal danced together perfectly. Before it was over, Cary had quit smiling.

By the intermission, Cary was scowling.

"How can you act like that?" Jane challenged him. "I did what you suggested. I got Neal a date. Can I help it if Toby can't dance?"

"Very clever," Cary said acidly. "You fix him up with the only girl in America who can't dance. That gives you a good excuse to show off with him every other dance."

"Show off!" Jane said. "That's mean!"

"You don't think it's mean to dance all night with your old boyfriend, while I'm on the bandstand and all my friends are just eating it up?"

He didn't come back again. Jane, her head high, fought tears the rest of the evening. "I know it's something I've done," Neal told Toby. "I'm really sorry."

"He's got a burr under his saddle," Toby said crossly. "The evening's almost over, anyway."

"I wish *you* had had a better time," Neal told her, frowning a little.

"Me?" Toby asked in amazement. "I loved it. I'm just sorry about Jane."

Cary had offered to drop the girls at Canby Hall after the dance and then take Neal to his train. But when Cary started acting as if he didn't know they were alive, Jane lost her temper. She found the public phone and called Alison back at Baker House. Alison listened quietly until Jane was all the way through.

"Let me get this straight," she said. "You'll take Neal to the station in a cab and then come home late. How about Toby?"

"Dee and her date will bring her home," Jane told her.

Alison sighed. "It sounds complicated, but workable. I can give you verbal permission for late return over the phone. Ring the front bell when you get here and I'll come down and let you in. As you know, you'll have to sign a special permission slip. Are you sure you can get a cab this late?"

"I *have* to," Jane told her.

"I can get to the train by myself," Neal protested when Jane told him what she had worked out.

"I don't want you to," she told him. "I have been a rotten hostess all day. The least I can do is see you off."

Neal laughed. "I always forget how stubborn you are. I love it."

Nothing was open in the village. Neal bought Jane and himself coffee from a machine in the train station. "You can't be serious about my not having had a good time," he told her. "Not only was it great to see you and meet your friends, but that Toby fascinates me. Everything about her is different from us, Jane. Meeting someone like that is a real experience."

Jane nodded. "She's not the only girl there who is that different," she told him, thinking about Dee, too. "I don't always know how to deal with them."

He looked at her curiously. "I bet they have the same problem with you."

She stared at him.

"In fact, it might be harder for them," he went on thoughtfully. "People who are used to blurting out exactly what they feel can't always tell what other people are *thinking*. Like Toby, I mean."

Jane nodded. He could be right about Toby . . . and Dee.

The sound of the train nearly drowned out his joking question. "Am I reading what *you're* thinking right now?"

She waited, half afraid. He must have been able to see how deeply she was hurt by Cary's neglect and anger. He rose and took her hands, drawing her to her feet. "I think I still see us as really good friends. I hope I'm right."

He hadn't tried to kiss her, and had only

put his arm around her when he first arrived. Like her mother said, "Neal is a gentleman."

She rose on tiptoe to press her lips to his cheek. "You are absolutely right," she whispered.

She had heard Neal tell the cab driver to wait for her until the train left. Not until she got to Canby Hall did she learn that he had also paid the driver for her ride home. Neal *was* a gentleman.

And then there was Cary.

When the cab stopped in the drive at Canby Hall, the watchman was making his rounds past Baker. He opened the cab door and let Jane out.

"Barrett?" he asked.

When Jane nodded, he pulled his keys from his pocket. "Miss Cavanaugh said to expect you. I'll let you in and call up to her. No point in her running down all those stairs."

Jane waited while he made the call and nodded goodnight. She decided there must have been a dorm party earlier, because the smell of popcorn was faint in the air.

The popcorn smell was no longer faint when she reached the fourth floor. All the doors along the hall were closed, including that of her own room. When she passed Dee and Maggie's room, the smell of popcorn almost knocked her over. Jane groaned silently. Using a hot plate in your room, or even an electric popper, was high crime and treason in a school with old buildings.

But when Dee got bored and restless, she never stopped to consider the punishment she could get. Like Neal had said, people that different were quite an experience!

Jane shrugged and went on up the stairs to Alison's floor.

CHAPTER SIXTEEN

Alison opened her door instantly to Jane's light knock. Doby rubbed against the leg of Alison's flowered lounging pajamas and purred up at Jane. "My goodness, something smells good," Alison said. "Come on in."

Alison had set the permit slip out on her low table. Her stereo was playing quietly in the background as she curled in the chair across from Jane. She laughed softly as she watched Jane sign her name. "What an evening you must have had! What threw your young man into his tantrum?"

Jane explained about Toby's not dancing and Cary's becoming steadily more jealous every time she and Neal danced together. "I couldn't just leave Neal standing there!" Jane told her.

"Of course you couldn't," Alison agreed.

Jane smiled in spite of herself. "I didn't think it was very funny while it was happening, but I guess Cary was acting pretty childish."

"I'm impressed," Alison told her. "I think you handled the entire affair very smoothly." As she spoke, she tilted her head and sniffed. "I know what I smell, popcorn. Doesn't it smell wonderful?"

Jane felt a thump in the pit of her stomach. Alison must *not* go looking for that popcorn. She wouldn't get past fourth floor before discovering that Dee (Jane was sure it was Dee's idea and not Maggie's) was flirting with trouble. "I don't smell a thing," Jane said, wishing her voice didn't sound so tense.

Alison laughed and rose. "You've been to Oakley Prep, and I know their parties . . . good food and *lots* of it. But I wasn't at the party and my stomach has forgotten dinner. Let's go down and invite ourselves for popcorn." She glanced down at her splashy lounging pajamas. "Maybe I better cover these crazy pajamas with something more housemotherly . . . like a robe."

For a moment Jane froze in panic. She had to warn Dee!

What was the matter with her? She didn't owe Dee anything. Dee hated her. Dee had the same as called her dishonest and unfair, as well as other names Jane had tried to forget. And Dee was a big girl who knew what she was doing.

But at the same time, Jane felt her heart

thumping wildly. Dee wasn't bad, she was only restless. The possible punishments Dee could get tumbled through Jane's head. It wasn't right. Dee couldn't help being herself and she shouldn't have to get into real trouble over it!

"I need to change into a robe, too," Jane said hastily, starting for the door.

"Wait up," Alison called from her closet. "I'll only take a moment."

"I'll meet you down there," Jane said, shoving Doby back inside the door and racing for the stairs.

Jane had never taken the stairs two at a time going down before. Only because Toby did it all the time was she sure it was even possible. Right away she realized she couldn't do it in heels. After the first two steps she kicked her shoes off and carried them to cut down on the clatter she was making.

The smell of popcorn was overpowering by the time she reached the fourth floor. She was breathless when she reached Dee and Maggie's room. She burst in without knocking to see a ring of astonished faces staring up at her. Everyone was there. Toby and Andy were perched on the beds, watching Dee and Maggie make popcorn on a hot plate on the floor. The room was noisy from the banging of the popcorn against the pot lid. Jane didn't dare shout, but they *had* to listen to her.

"Listen to me!" she whispered urgently. "Quick! Somebody grab that popcorn and run down to the kitchen. You, Maggie, get that hot plate out of sight. Now!" She knew she sounded like a drill sergeant from an old army movie but she couldn't help it. They just kept on staring at her with open mouths. "Hurry!" Jane insisted. "Alison is putting on her robe this very minute to come down for some popcorn."

"How did she know?" Dee asked. "Who told her?"

"Not me," Jane said, returning her glare. "She smelled it, how else? Hurry up!"

For a moment, Dee stood with her mouth firm, as if she might decide that getting into trouble was just what she wanted.

"Dee," Jane said softly. "THINK!"

Maggie was thinking. She swiftly unplugged the hot plate and set it inside the closet. After a long glance at Jane, Dee rose, lifting the pan with the popcorn still banging away against its tin lid.

"Go!" Jane ordered. "Run downstairs to the kitchen; turn the burner on high so the stove will be hot!"

Andy tumbled off the bed and went over to help Dee. "We'll never get away with it; smell this place!"

"Just go!" Jane insisted. Then she groaned. "Faster. I hear her coming."

Maggie ran ahead to get the small stove turned on. Andy and Dee together carried the hot pot toward the stairs. As they started down, Toby raced out the door and started upstairs.

"Where are you going?" Jane whispered frantically.

"I'm going to cut off Alison at the pass," Toby called back in that put-on Western drawl.

Jane looked around the room frantically. Andy was right. The smell of popcorn was overwhelming. "Perfume!" she whispered. "Surely someone has spray perfume."

Her own perfume wouldn't spray. It was French and kept in a little crystal bottle with a glass stopper and a wand. She looked for her spray deodorant and couldn't even find that. In desperation, she grabbed the spray bottle off Andy's dresser and started back to Dee's room.

Only then did she remember her robe. She had forgotten to change after darting away from Alison. She grabbed her robe from the floor and dragged it behind her.

With one hand, Jane sprayed the room steadily with great clouds of fragrance. With her free hand, she unzipped her skirt, kicked it out of her way, and started wriggling into her robe. The perfume was so heavy in the air that she had to hold her breath to keep from sneezing. If she hadn't been trying not to sneeze, she would have broken up with laughter. Spraying the air around herself steadily, she felt like a fireboat in Boston Harbor.

Toby had disappeared but Jane heard her voice. She sounded very close, just above at the top of the stairs. When Jane finally struggled all the way into her robe, she tiptoed out into the hall and pulled Dee and Maggie's door shut behind her. She ran on tiptoe down the stairs toward the kitchen, spraying the perfume wildly into the popcorn smell in the air as she went.

Toby met Alison coming down the stairs.

"Oh, hi!" she said, standing directly in Alison's path.

"Hi, yourself," Alison said, stopping to look at her curiously. "What's up?"

"Oh, nothing," Toby said. "I . . . I just thought I'd come up and meet you. Jane said you were on your way down."

"So I was," Alison said, starting past her. "Let's go."

"This very minute?" Toby asked, edging into her path again.

"What are we waiting for?" Alison asked.

Toby's inspiration came like one of those light bulbs over a character's head in a cartoon. "Aren't you going to bring Doby?" Toby asked.

Alison laughed. "I *do* sometimes go out without my cat." Her tone was playfully sarcastic.

"But cats *love* popcorn," Toby said. "My cats back home just adore it."

"I thought your cats back home were barn

cats," Alison said, studying Toby's face.

"They start that way," Toby said earnestly. "But then I bring them in the house. . . ."

"And teach them to eat popcorn," Alison said. "Toby, you are not yourself tonight."

Toby wilted. "I guess I'm not. It's been a really strange evening. You do realize that was my first date. And my first dance." She paused.

Alison put her arm around Toby's shoulder. "Just because you had a strange evening, you think I should have one, too? You really think I should take Doby along when I go to crash a popcorn party?"

"I'll even carry him," Toby offered eagerly. "I know he'll just love it."

Alison turned and started back up the stairs. "Okay, I give in. I guess I've done crazier things. I just can't remember when."

The moment Alison opened her door, Doby was there. When Toby leaned to pick him up, Alison laughed. "That big lazy cat can just walk like the rest of us."

"He'll go too fast," Toby said, holding him against her shoulder.

"Too fast for what?" Alison asked.

"Dancing is very tiring work," Toby replied, clinging to the cat and walking down the stairs carefully, one step at a time.

"I thought you didn't dance."

Toby buried her scarlet face in Doby's fur. "It's even tiring to watch," she explained.

When they reached the fourth floor, Alison frowned. "Whew!" she said. "Somebody must have spilled her perfume."

"Really?" Toby said, trying to keep from gasping.

"There's something very strange here," Alison mused. "I don't understand how I could smell popcorn clear upstairs and only smell perfume down here."

"*I* smell popcorn," Toby said.

Even Alison smelled it again when they reached the main floor. She could also hear it just beginning to bang away at the lid of the pot, while Maggie melted butter for the bowl they had already filled.

"Welcome!" Dee called as Toby and Alison appeared in the doorway. "Good, you brought Doby." As she spoke, she leaned and picked a buttery kernel from the bowl and offered it to the cat. He sniffed it, angled his head, took it between his back teeth, and crunched loudly.

"Okay, you win," Alison laughed. "Toby said he would like it but I wasn't at all sure. I hope you don't have to be a cat to get a bowl of that wonderful-smelling stuff."

She settled on a stool and watched them finish the second panful. "Who spilled her perfume up on fourth?" she asked. "You need a gas mask to breathe in that hall."

"It was Andy's," Jane said swiftly, meeting Andy's eye warily.

"Whatever it is, it's powerful stuff!" Alison said.

Andy smiled. "I've never thought of it as powerful," she said. "Actually, it's called Sweet Innocence."

Dee nearly choked on her popcorn at Andy's words.

CHAPTER
SEVENTEEN

After Neal's visit, Jane felt numb and defeated. She got a sweet thank you note from him, which only plunged her into guilt. How could she be so crazy about someone as childish as Cary, and not be captivated by someone as nice as Neal? Especially since Cary hated her and Neal obviously loved her? Her mother wrote that she and Neal had had "a nice talk. Your friend October impressed Neal so much. You must bring her home and let us meet her."

Of all the girls in 407, Andy had been the least involved in the events of that weekend, unless you wanted to count having her perfume sacrificed to the cause of saving Dee's skin. Yet in the days following, Andy was the most changed. All the change was for the better. Her old sunny nature began to come back. She teased and laughed and even looked different, her eyes glowing with warmth.

"Of course I've noticed!" Toby told Jane.

"I haven't even asked myself why, I've just basked in it, like a lizard on a sunny rock."

Maggie looked up from her book. "If you think Andy is changed *here,* you should see her at practice. She doesn't even touch the ground in her leaps. More often than not, she gets applause when she finishes her solo."

"We need to go watch her," Jane said. "I'd like to see her dance, wouldn't you, Toby?"

Maggie frowned. "The production is so close now, I'd wait for dress rehearsal. They're finishing up the costumes now and they're spectacular."

Andy never walked from Baker over to the auditorium without remembering the lecture Faith had given her on that same path. She had been angry at first, convinced that Faith was simply echoing Canby Hall propaganda because it was easier to join them than it was to lick them.

She even went out of her way to watch the lead dancer, Ari, perform, to convince herself that she had been discriminated against. In one way, that had been a mistake. She had been forced to face the fact that Ari *was* good. Ari really *was* better than she was. The other thing she realized was that Ari's role was not as exciting as some of the dances in the chorus. Ari had one great dream sequence with the prince and the wakening scene, but Andy's routines were more dramatic and there were more of them.

Once she realized this, she really began to work. The smatterings of applause that had come at almost every practice grew longer and more enthusiastic. What a ham I am, she said to herself. Give me thirty seconds of praise and I'll kill myself! Within a week, the director stopped her as she was leaving and patted her shoulder. "You're the most improved dancer we have, Cord. And when you really smile, Matt doesn't even need to use that floodlight."

"Matt?" she asked, confused.

He motioned to the light booth at the rear of the auditorium and she glanced up. The Oakley Prep boy working the lights was looking down. He waved, smiling. She mumbled some sort of thanks and got out in a hurry, realizing that the applause had always started up there. And his name was Matt.

The pumpkin bars came from Chicago the same day the costumes were fitted. "My favorites!" Andy wailed. "But I don't dare touch them if I want that costume to keep on fitting."

"Costume?" Jane said, looking up. "Toby and I are just waiting for the dress rehearsal to come see you dance. What color is your costume?"

"A pale soft gold," Andy said.

"She looks like the flame of a candle in it," Maggie said.

"Get thee behind me, pumpkin bars," Andy

groaned. "I could turn into a full blown camp fire with three or four of those. It's dinner time, where's Toby? Don't tell me she's closing up the library again."

"She already did that," Maggie said. "She was talking on the phone when I went through the lobby."

"Phone?" Andy said. "Toby never talks on the phone."

"Today she does."

Toby found the phone number in her box when she came in from the library. She frowned at it a long time. There wasn't any name on it, just a local number. Finally curiosity won. When a man's voice answered, she almost hung up. "October Houston here," she managed to say.

"Toby! I was waiting for your call."

She recognized Randy's voice only when he spoke her name. "Listen, Toby," he went on. "I've been thinking. Can you skip dinner? If so, I'll buy you a hamburger at the diner. I want to talk to you about something."

Toby was speechless for a long moment. "I guess," she finally said.

"Hey," he said quickly. "Don't get the wrong idea. I'm not into cradle-robbing. This isn't a date or anything like that. I just thought we could catch a sandwich while I run my bright idea past you. I could be by in five minutes. Want to watch outside?"

Not into cradle-robbing! There was a man

who could win trophies for tact. She sighed. But her birthday was almost there. Maybe a year would make a difference.

Randy rattled to a stop in his father's truck and leaned over to shove the door open.

"Now what's this all about?" she asked before she got the door shut.

He grinned over at her. "Wait till we get food," he said. "I'm starving. Hey! Good to see you. I haven't seen you for weeks except that day we played tennis."

"A girl can drown in paper," she told him. "I almost blew my studies and have been grinding to catch up."

"I know how that is." He laughed. "I pulled that same trick my junior year. Barely got off probation in time."

She grinned at him. It was good to hear she wasn't the only one that stupid. By the time he filled her in about the progress of the new stables and described a colt his father wanted to buy, they were in town.

Cary was behind the counter in the diner. When Toby barely nodded at him, Randy looked surprised. "Don't you like your roommate's friend?"

"He isn't my roommate's friend anymore," she said. "Cheeseburger medium rare with fries and a Coke. Now what did you have to talk about?"

He laughed, signaled for Cary and gave the order. "Boy, are you into impatience! I wanted to talk to you about tennis. You have real natural talent. I know you worked awfully steady and awfully hard to move your game from nothing to where you were the other day, but hard work alone won't do that, Toby."

She shook her head. "Sweat," she told him. "Once in about a blue moon a shot really feels good."

He nodded. "That's because you know instinctively how a shot is supposed to feel. A lot of people never figure it out. Believe me, Toby, I've been around this game a long time."

She looked at him as Cary set their order down. "So why are you telling me all this?"

"I want you to try out for the team."

"Oh no." She shook her head. "I'm a beginner. Those girls have years on me. I don't have a chance to make that team."

"I didn't say I thought you'd make it," he said.

She stared at him. "What kind of a friend are you? You want me to try out for a team you know I won't make? That's crazy."

He shook his head. "Listen to me. You can't just learn from a coach. You won't ever know how good you are until you compete against the best around. And you need to let them see that you're someone to beat. The minute you play against those girls, you will have partners available. Another year, you'll have a slot."

She ate slowly. "This is really strange,

Randy. Why does it matter to you?"

He laughed. "For starters, I guess I thought we were friends." He paused. "But there is something else, too. When I first caught tennis fever, I hung back just like you're doing. It took an older player to bully me into trying out for the team."

"Why did he have to do that when you have such a good game?" she asked.

"I'm better now than I was then, but the real reason I wouldn't go out was that I really hated the guts of one of the ranked players. He had baited me and made my life miserable for years. My friend figured out that the thought of his beating me was keeping me out of tennis."

When she was silent for a moment, he finished off his French fries and laughed. "You're being awfully quiet."

She shrugged and grinned at him. "Would you believe that I see the name GIGI NORTON written inside my head?"

"I'd believe that." He grinned.

"So maybe you're right. Maybe I'll give it a shot."

Dee Adams was talking to Cary as they started toward the register. "Hi, Toby . . . Randy," she said. "You wouldn't be on your way back to Baker, would you? I'm in the market for a ride."

"Hop aboard if you're not too proud to ride in a truck," Randy said.

"Pride's not my problem." She laughed.

"Want to discuss your problems with Uncle Ran here?" He laughed as both girls squeezed into the seat beside him.

"Toby knows," Dee said.

Toby listened to Dee and Randy kid each other as the truck wound back to the campus. Would she ever learn to make such easy conversation with a guy? She thought about Neal and how comfortable she had been with him after the tennis match. But that had been a fluke.

Randy let them out right at the door of Baker. As the truck pulled away with Randy waving back, Toby turned to Dee. "What do I know?"

Dee frowned a moment, then realized what Toby was after. "Oh, my problem? How I'm the world's prize know-it-all? You saw all the stuff I dumped on Jane, and the names I called her. I was so sure my way was right and hers was wrong. Then who knocks herself out to save my skin the other night? Who else but cool Jane. But she's so in control I don't know how to let her know how much I appreciate it . . . short of crawling on my knees, that is."

"Just tell her," Toby suggested.

Dee shook her head. "She'd just nod," Dee said. "I want her to really believe me."

A cold gray rain began early on the day of the final tryouts for the tennis team. The weather didn't really matter since the matches were

scheduled on indoor courts anyway, but the
sullen sky put Toby into the same mood.

I don't even know why I'm doing this, Toby
told herself.

When she got to the courts, Dee was already
there, hitting balls with another girl. When
the rally ended, Dee came to the end of the
court and called Toby over. "I thought you
had put all this behind you."

Toby could only shrug. "So what's to lose?"
she asked.

Dee grinned and shrugged.

Competing against other players with the
coach and a group of other adults watching
changed the game. Toby felt that same stiff
self-consciousness that had ruined her first
set against Neal and Jane. Since the players
were rotated after each game, Toby came up
against Dee after losing her first two games.

"Hey, relax," Dee said.

"You mean it's not Wimbledon?" Toby
laughed, remembering that other match.

"Exactly that," Dee said. "And if it isn't
fun, go find a horse."

Playing against Dee *was* fun. She was swift
as a deer and her deep shots so forceful that
Toby had to fight to get to the net. Although
Dee finally beat her, it was anything but a
rout. The score went to six games even with
Dee beating her in the play-off.

Then Toby was across the net from Gigi
Norton.

Gigi's expression was the hard part. She

stood in perfect waiting position, almost sneering across the net at Toby. Naturally Toby hit both serves into the net, losing the point. When Gigi won her own serve, making her two games against Toby's none, Toby was ready to give up.

Randy had told her it was typical of a beginning player to have trouble with the serve. "With you it's either win or lose," he laughed. "That'll change, don't worry."

Toby's first serve was a winning one. She saw Gigi move back and felt a flush of pride. She had earned that one moment of grudging respect at least. The next serve was not a winner but was strong and deep. Gigi's return was weak enough to allow Toby to reach the net for a volley and a point. Something bright and warm exploded in Toby's chest. She could do it. Maybe not all the time, but it was there deep down, the ability to play the way Dee did, fast and loose and not missing an opportunity.

Gigi won the set at six-four and shook hands silently, turning away without a word.

By the time the games were over, Toby's legs ached in a dull hot way. She must have run a thousand miles up to that net and back. Punch and cookies were served in the social room while the scores were tallied. A number of the girls Toby had played against came up to talk to her. The tall blond girl who had wiped up the court with Toby in the first game, came up grinning. "Hey," she said. "I'm Midge Forester. Good playing. Like to hit balls some time?"

"I'd like to," Toby said, hearing Randy's voice in the back of her mind, saying, "The minute you play against those girls, you will have partners available. You can't just learn from a coach. You need to let them see that you're someone to beat."

She and Midge talked while they demolished the plate of cookies. Midge was from Florida and, like Dee, had played since she was a little kid. "In a way, you have the advantage," Midge told her. "Sometimes I get bored with it, and feel like I have been picking up little green balls all my life. That probably won't happen to you."

"Not for a long time yet," Toby agreed.

The coach came in and announced rankings of the team. Dee would play second singles, and Gigi third. When Toby's name wasn't on the list, Dee edged over to stand by her.

"You'll have another chance next year," she whispered to Toby. "You'll make it in a breeze." She paused. "That is, if you want to."

Toby nodded. "I want to."

"And you're okay now?" Dee asked softly.

Toby grinned at her. "I knew I wouldn't make it. In a way I'm glad. Like you say, there's always next year."

The coach was there, shaking Toby's hand and saying encouraging things about her game. On the way back to Baker, Dee shook her head. "I can't believe you can play that well without being hooked on the game."

"I am hooked," Toby admitted. "And I probably should admit that Randy bullied me into that tryout."

Dee stopped in the path. "Don't tell me you're still just out to impress that guy!"

"Hey," Toby told her. "Didn't you ever go to the store for a loaf of bread and come home with a dozen other things? I went out for tennis because of Randy. I'm staying in it for myself."

"I'm sorry you won't be on the team, for my own fun," Dee said.

"I will be," Toby told her. "Next year!"

It really *was* better that she hadn't made the team. She needed time to sell her dad on tennis. He wasn't ready to understand how chasing a ball around could be more important to her than grades.

CHAPTER EIGHTEEN

Dee brought the package up from the desk and stuck her head in the door. "Goodies for Andrea Cord," she called. Then, looking around, "Where is she?"

"In the shower trying to drown her butterflies."

Dee stared at her, confused.

"Tonight's the dress rehearsal," Jane reminded her. "Andy won't admit being nervous, but did you see her swallow a bite of her dinner tonight?"

As she spoke, Andy came in, bundled in her pink terrycloth robe. "Care package," Dee told her, leaving. "I put it on your desk."

Andy groaned. "There is no way I can put anything into this stomach. But you guys open it if you want. Just save me some for after the rehearsal."

Toby rose and went to the desk. She stared at the package a minute. "Hey," she said.

"This isn't from Chicago. It's from some fancy store in Philadelphia."

Andy, with her warm-ups half on, went over to look. "You have to be kidding. I don't know anybody in Philadelphia." She frowned at the address label. "Andrea Cord. That's me, I guess."

"Wow!" Jane said, before the wrapping was all the way off. "I recognize the box already. That's my mother's favorite brand of French chocolates. Do you ever rate!"

"But why would your mother send me chocolates?"

Toby read the small square gift card tucked under the ribbon and giggled. "If these are from Mrs. Barrett, she's too shy to sign her name."

"Give me that," Andy ordered, taking the card from her. She stood frowning, reading it for herself. "I don't get this."

"You could let us help. What does it say?" Jane asked.

"For the secret star," Andy said quietly.

"With no name?" Jane asked.

Andy shook her head.

"Hey!" Toby cried. "You have a fan."

"Impossible," Andy said, putting the card down. "And on second thought, don't open the box until we get back." She paused. "Are you all sure you want to sit through this rehearsal?"

"I'm really sick about this," Toby said. "I want to come, but I can't. You wouldn't believe how much I have to do in these two hours. But I'll be there opening night, no matter what!"

Andy nodded. "Gosh, I hope you understand," Toby said.

Andy shrugged. "You know what you have to do."

"I'm coming," Jane said, grinning at Andy. "I have to be there. As my mother could tell you, I can't be trusted alone here with that box of chocolates!"

The mysterious box of candy was actually helpful. Andy kept wondering about it instead of worrying about her performance. As she stood in the dressing room, holding up her arms for the glorious silken gold dress to drop over her head, she found herself smiling. Maybe she didn't want to know who her fan was. Maybe it was just enough to have someone think of her like that . . . as a secret star. She had just finished dressing when Maggie stuck her head in. "Come quick, Andy, while the doors are still closed. I want you to see how great the set looks finished and lighted."

Maggie took Andy's hand and led her swiftly down the steps to the orchestra of the auditorium. "Now don't look around until we're halfway to the back," Maggie warned. As Maggie stopped, Andy glanced up at the light booth where Matt was adjusting streams of tinted light onto the set behind her.

"Now look," Maggie whispered. Before

Andy could turn, a beam of pale lemon-colored light strayed from the stage to pin Andy there in the aisle. As she and Maggie both stared up in astonishment, Andy saw Matt smiling down at her. As she watched, he raised his right hand in a sign of triumph.

Matt. At that moment Andy knew. Matt had sent the candy. Matt, who had applauded her solo every single practice. She smiled shyly, ducking her head, before turning at Maggie's tug on her arm.

She gasped. The sets that she knew were cardboard and stapled fabric had been transformed by the skill of Maggie and her crew and the streams of light into a medieval wonderland. The stones of the castle wall cast proper shadows and the green of the meadows looked as inviting as real grass. "It's wonderful!" Andy cried, clasping her hands together.

Andy glanced quickly back up at Matt's booth, but he was gone and Maggie had her hand, dragging her away.

The director was dancing with nervousness as the audience filed into the brightly lit auditorium. Andy, peering with other dancers through slits in the curtain, watched the people take their places. Alison Cavanaugh came in with her friend Michael, and Andy saw with horror that the headmistress, Patrice Allardyce, was with a group of stiffly clad people she suspected were trustees. Why was

she doing this to herself? Every familiar face
sent a ripple of ice up her spine.

Maybe it was a good thing Toby had to
grind away at the books, although Andy's
feelings had been hurt that she couldn't spare
this *one* evening to come with Jane.

Jane! Andy gasped when she saw that
familiar blond head turned at the doorway.
Cary. Jane had come with Cary. That wasn't
possible. Jane hadn't mentioned Cary's name
or been near the diner, or had a phone call
from him since That Weekend. Before Andy
recovered from her shock, someone touched
her back. "Places, dancers," the director ordered, and a wave of applause signaled that
the orchestra leader was walking to the
podium.

Oh please, Andy told herself breathlessly.
Oh please, let everything be right!

With the opening strains of music, Andy
began to relax. As the curtain whispered back
and she heard the gasp of delight from the
audience, she felt a surge of excitement. Then
the flood of light dimmed and the spotlight
moved to where she and her partner were
posed. She rose slowly in the double warmth
of the spotlight and the caring hand behind it.

Never mind who was the princess. She was
Matt's secret star.

Jane had hoped she could walk over to the
dress rehearsal with Dee. Maggie and Andy

had left early and Toby was buried in her books by the time Jane was ready, but Dee was nowhere to be found.

"So I walk alone, not a big deal," Jane told Toby as she put on her coat. "Sure you won't relent and come along?"

"Positive," Toby told her. "Clap for me, too."

It was just chilly enough for Jane's breath to make a cloud around her face as she let herself out of Baker House. The night was so quiet that she could hear the distant barking of a dog somewhere off beyond the campus. She walked swiftly even though she had plenty of time to see the curtain come up. Between Maggie's excitement over the stage scenery and Andy's part in the performance, she was really excited about the evening. Besides, she had done nothing but work since Neal left.

When Cary called to her, she paused only a second before walking on swiftly. What was this going to be? Another of those talks that ended in anger? Another chance for him to scold her for things that weren't even her fault?

His footsteps echoed as he ran to catch up with her and grab her arm.

"Let go or I'll scream," she said quietly.

His hand dropped. "Come on, Jane," he said. "I want to apologize."

She kept walking. Let him talk. No gentleman would behave the way he had and then expect a few words of apology to make it all right again. She was writer enough to have his script already written in her mind. He was only jealous because he liked her. Blat. Blat. Blat.

"You don't have to listen," he said. "But I have to say this. You don't even have to make up with me. But I have to tell you what I think."

When no answer came, he continued to run along beside her, trying to see into her face. If anyone saw them she would die of embarrassment. "This is ridiculous," she told him hotly.

"Of course it is," he panted. "Stop and give me one minute, and I'll let you alone."

She stopped. "I have a second hand on my watch," she told him, not caring how cold it sounded.

"Oh, Jane!" He sighed. "Okay, one minute. I made a mistake. I treated you unfairly. BIG mistake. But then I didn't know as much about you then as I do now."

She looked at him, astonished. New script. What was this all about?

"I knew you were pretty, and fun to be with, all in your own low-key way. I didn't realize what else you are. That Neal would be a jerk not to fight for you. And I would be, too."

"What is this?" she asked, touched more than she wanted to admit by his words.

"You," he said. "Your friend Dee came in the other day. We were just talking, you know,

when she started telling me this funny story,
strictly slapstick comedy, about how you
ripped into her room, ordered everybody
around, sprayed the world with perfume, and
saved her neck. I was laughing myself silly
until she got to the punch line."

"Punch line?" Jane asked, not sure she
wanted to hear it.

He took her hands. "I think I have her
words right. Dee said, 'And this from a girl I
have bullied and beaten up on with my mouth
since the day we met.' "

Jane dropped her eyes. "It's just Dee's
way."

"That's what I'm saying, Jane," Cary
whispered. "Only a really great person would
understand that and lift a hand to save the
other girl's skin."

He was smiling down into her face. She
wanted to hug him. Instead she dropped her
eyes. "My minute is up," he said quietly. "But
I do want to warn you that I'm no stupider
than Cornelius Worthington the Third.
There is no way I'm going to give up on you,
Jane Barrett."

She wanted to cry.

"Truce?" he asked.

"Truce," she whispered.

He tucked her hand under his arm. "Okay.
I took the night off to see you. Where were
we going in such a hurry before I got that
off my chest?"

"Andy's rehearsal," she gasped, with sudden

panic. "Hurry, we have to see the opening curtain."

Before the final curtain even went down on the closing dance, the audience was on its feet. In the wings, Andy shivered with delight at the waves of clapping and some man's voice shouting, "Bravo! Bravo!"

The curtain calls seemed to go on forever. Andy swept to the floor in each bow, feeling as if she could fly with happiness. When the director finally came to the stage and quieted the audience, he was beaming with pleasure. "Save your applause for opening night," he told the audience. "And tell your friends that this *Sleeping Beauty* is an event they can't afford to miss."

He got a good hand as the curtain drew shut behind him and the auditorium was flooded with light.

Andy carefully fitted the beautiful gold costume onto its hanger and put her own clothes back on. She paused in the doorway to pull on her angora cap. The paths that led from the auditorium were filled with people walking along in little groups, chattering noisily. She was on the bottom step when Matt stepped from the shadows. When he stood that close to her he looked taller than he did up there in the light control booth. He was really slender, with glowing dark skin under a plaid cap that matched his scarf. His smile was the best, wide and warm and shy all at once.

"Congratulations," he said, smiling at her. "You were really super."

"Thank you," she said, hoping her voice didn't sound sappy. "You were wonderful yourself. Everything was wonderful."

He nodded. "It's been great all along, but everything really came together tonight." He hesitated. "I can only think of one thing that would make this evening greater. . . . Can I walk back with you?"

Even if she hadn't liked the way he looked and sounded, she might have agreed because of how obviously he was afraid she'd say no. She grinned at him. "Who am I to spoil your wonderful evening?"

The rest of the crowd was well ahead of them as they started toward Baker House. Since he couldn't seem to think of anything to say, she looked over at him. "So you're from Philadelphia," she said brightly.

"How did you know that?" He sounded genuinely surprised.

"Just a good guess. That's where the candy came from."

"I hoped you'd guess," he admitted. "That was true, you know. I really meant it. And you're from Chicago," he said, then laughed. "I asked around."

The walk was all too short. By the time they talked a little about the play and their hometowns and their personal theatrical ambitions, the front door of Baker House was right there.

Just as they paused at the steps, a falling star streaked across the sky. Andy, startled, put her hand on Matt's arm. He covered it with his own.

"Where I come from, you get a wish for every falling star," Matt whispered.

For some silly reason, Andy couldn't meet his eyes and only nodded. He smiled and leaned to touch her lips lightly.

CHAPTER NINETEEN

Andy liked getting compliments, but just that once, she would have been glad to find the lobby empty. But Alison was there, waiting to tell her now spectacular the rehearsal had been. "I wish someone had videotaped it," Alison added. "I would love to play it over and over." She grinned. "I guess I'll have to come every night and memorize it."

When Andy was finally free to go on upstairs, her impulse was to dance all the way. Room 407 was silent when Andy opened the door. Jane was sitting on her bed with her scarf half off, staring into space. Guess what that's all about, Andy laughed to herself. Should I wake her up out of that dream and find out how she and Cary got together again?

Toby, surrounded by books, looked up and smiled. "I understand I missed the greatest Canby Hall show ever."

"It was wonderful from my side of the

lights," Andy admitted, pirouetting around the room. "I had a wonderful night!"

"Me, too," Jane said quietly.

Toby glanced at both of them and smiled.

"I had a pretty good night myself," she said quietly.

"All by yourself studying?" Andy asked, stopping by her desk. "I doesn't sound that great."

"Well, I didn't study *all* the time," Toby said.

"Look at her," Andy told Jane. "Look at those eyes. Something is going on. She's up to something. Come on now, Toby."

Toby tried desperately to keep a straight face, but burst into laughter. At the sound, the door opened and Dee's head popped in. "Ready now?" she asked.

"Ready for what?" Jane asked, staring up at her.

As Jane spoke, Dee reached in, snapped off the light, and plunged the room into darkness. Light blazed up at once from the doorway, as Dee entered carrying a large cake completely covered with blazing candles. As soon as she was inside the door, Dee began to sing and a chorus of voices sounded from the hall outside.

"Happy Birthday to you, Happy Birthday to You, Happy Birthday, dear October. . . ."

The little room was suddenly crammed with people, Alison and Maggie and all the girls along the hall who had become friends in those swift weeks. They were singing so loudly that they almost drowned out Andy and Jane's cries. "It can't be," Jane wailed.

"But it is!" Andy corrected her. "It's October. Why in the world would anybody be named after a month she wasn't *born* in?"

Toby had leaped to her feet. With shining eyes, she blew out every candle with a single breath.

Andy collapsed backward on her bed with a groan. "It's your birthday, Toby, your very own birthday, and we didn't know it! Toby, how can you ever forgive us?"

"Forgive nothing!" Toby drawled. "When I realized I was where nobody knew it was my birthday, I almost split. All my life I wanted to plan a surprise party and never had a chance. Now I did it!"

"But, Toby," Jane cried. "How can you surprise yourself with a party?"

Toby grinned and put an arm around both Andy and Jane. "Never underestimate a Texan," she drawled. "This birthday is the biggest surprise of my life! Like I told Dad when I got permission to order all this stuff, 'Can you believe it, Dad? I not only live with people. I even like it.' "

Andy and Jane looked at each other and then at Toby. "You don't like it any more than we do," Andy told her, with Jane nodding in agreement.

"Less talk and more cake," Dee demanded loudly, handing Toby the knife and holding out her plate.

"Hear, hear!" Maggie called from behind her.

"I hope there will be popcorn," Alison said quietly. "I brought Doby along just in case."

Dee looked up, startled to see the housemother smile at her as she passed her plate for cake.

Over the candles, Toby and Andrea and Jane exchanged looks. Looks that said, This is the beginning of something good.

"Happy Birthday, October," Andy said.

"Happy Birthday, Toby," Jane said.

"Happy Birthday to friendship," Toby whispered.

What happens when Shelley, Faith, and Dana come back to Canby Hall to help celebrate Alison's wedding — and Toby, Andy, and Jane wish they hadn't? Read The Girls of Canby Hall #20, SOMETHING OLD, SOMETHING NEW, to find out.

Read All About
The Girls of Canby Hall!